"Ms. Mann, I'm your friend."

And I'm your slave, Sarina thought, gazing into the warm, penetrating eyes of the man standing in her office. Suddenly she realized what he meant. "Oh, you mean you're my friend." Her eyes popped. "*You're* my rent-a-friend?"

"That's right," Max replied.

Sarina's mouth fell open. "There must be some mistake," she said, retreating behind her desk. "You're a man." Her eyes met his espresso gaze, drinking in the heat. *And a gorgeous man, too.*

"It just so happened that I shared your areas of expertise and interests, so I was assigned to you."

Sarina sank into her chair. She could think of a number of assignments for Max, but none of them had anything to do with friendship!

Dear Reader,

I'm pleased to welcome back Lori Copeland with *Fudgeballs and Other Sweets*. She is one of the original launch authors for Love & Laughter as well as an award-winning author for writing humor. *Publishers Weekly* had this to say recently about her work: "Copeland has a winner in this crisply written, sweetly sentimental tale of love lost and found." With Lori's name on the cover, you know you're in for a good read and a good time! Plus the story features two cute and memorable dogs—could you ask for more?

Valerie Kirkwood also has written her second book for us, *Rent-a-Friend*. The poor heroine has been badly betrayed by her best friend, and she's vowed not to have any more friends—*ever*! But that just doesn't work, so she decides to take the intelligent route, one most women can relate to very easily: she goes *shopping* for a friend.

As an interesting aside, both Lori and Valerie also write historical romances. Clearly a talented pair!

So relax and enjoy a chuckle.

Malle Vallik

Malle Vallik
Associate Senior Editor

RENT-A-FRIEND
Valerie Kirkwood

Harlequin Books

TORONTO • NEW YORK • LONDON
AMSTERDAM • PARIS • SYDNEY • HAMBURG
STOCKHOLM • ATHENS • TOKYO • MILAN
MADRID • WARSAW • BUDAPEST • AUCKLAND

ISBN 0-373-44042-1

RENT-A-FRIEND

Copyright © 1998 by Valerie Kane

Printed in U.S.A.

A funny thing happened...

The conventional wisdom is that we should take more time to smell the roses. I've always suspected this advice came to us from the makers of allergy medications, and have generally preferred laughter as my antidote to sneezing and wheezing, instead. I suppose that's because my childhood allergies often kept me indoors, where, after demonstrating to Mother that dusting—and just about every other form of housework—caused coughing fits worthy of Camille, I'd click on the TV for a dose of those fabulous screwball comedies of the thirties and forties. Zany plots, urbane dialogue, and (sigh) a screen filled with Joel McCrae's shoulders. (*The Palm Beach Story*, 1942. Check it out.) How lucky could a congested romance writer-in-training get?

When you consider that these film gems were written against the backdrop of a global depression and war, do you wonder, as I do, what all the current whining is about? That's why I say, stop worrying about the roses your nose will never meet! Tune out the talk shows and the women who are addicted to electrolysis. Just throw back your head and laugh. I hope *Rent-A-Friend* helps you to do just that.

Gesundheit!

—Valerie Kirkwood

Books by Valerie Kirkwood

HARLEQUIN LOVE & LAUGHTER
20—ACCIDENTALLY YOURS

For my best guyfriend, Lary Crews

Special thanks to Laurie Bisig and Nancy Vinsel,
who gave me New York; Giam Paolo Bianconcini,
who gave me Italy; and Alan Kane who gives me
the world.

Prologue

SARINA MANN DOKTER had been sitting in the deep whirl-pool tub so long, all that remained of once-majestic mountains of bubbles were soap slicks skimming the chill water. Either she had just married the most patient man in the world, or Rance had dashed out to perform an emergency tummy tuck.

Or maybe he'd just dashed out. Perhaps while waiting for her to come out of the bathroom, he'd replayed the moment she'd been about to take her wedding vows, when she'd asked the priest to repeat the question.

"Sarina, what part of 'until death do you part' don't you understand?" Father DeGrasso had asked.

Impatiently pushing poufs of tulle away from her ear as though they stood between her and happily-ever-after, she'd forced a lame smile and said, "Sorry, Father. It's this blasted veil." Then, summoning a breath, "Of course, I do."

Obviously, she'd convinced her pastor that she'd had no doubts—she was married. But had she convinced poor Rance?

"Dear, are you sure you want to do this?" he had asked when he'd awakened her with a phone call that morning.

A vice president at a multinational investment firm, Sarina had a reputation as a bold risk-taker who refused to second-guess her gutsy decisions. Certainly, her soon-to-be husband ought to have known her better than to ask if she had any last-minute doubts. Unless...

"Aren't *you* sure, Rance?"

"Uh-uh, muffin," he'd cautioned. "I asked you first."

Pausing, Sarina had glanced at the hand-beaded gown hanging on her closet door. She'd once joked to Rance that it had cost her the equivalent of the gross national product of a tiny third-world country. He had to realize, as anyone who knew her should, that she could never have indulged in such extravagance unless she believed she would be taking her one and only trip down the aisle. Making a perturbed face, she'd said, "You can't possibly doubt my sincerity, darling."

"I'm not doubting your sincerity, sweet," he'd replied. "I know there isn't a duplicitous bone in your body. I'm only asking because I want you to know that nothing matters to me but your happiness." Rance's voice had turned to brandy—warm, smooth, comforting. "And if you should have a change of heart, dearest, even as you walk down the aisle, I'll understand and gladly step aside."

He was so good to her. So selfless, so thoughtful. So why was she sitting in a tub of ice water on her wedding night, wondering whether or not she had been right to marry him? Even her best friend, Jillian, who still behaved guardedly around Rance, claimed her only grounds for mistrust were that he was too good to be true—wealthy, gorgeous, and one of the most sought-after plastic surgeons in New York.

"I don't trust a man who has no discernible faults. It isn't natural," Jillian had told Sarina after first meeting Rance. "On the other hand, he can liposuction me anytime he wants."

Sarina laughed now as she had then, confident that the last thing that would ever come between her and her best friend was a man.

When she and Jillian had met that summer in Rome, two American students sharing a room in a *pensione,* they had been little more than cordial to one another. Soon after,

Sarina began dating Giorgio, one of the legion of Roman men with a gaze that can make love to a woman in ways she'll remember for the rest of her life. A month later, believing she was in love, Sarina was ready for more than his gaze. Then, a pained and uncertain Jillian revealed that she'd not only seen Giorgio with two other American women, but that he'd asked *her* out as well. Naturally, she had said, she'd told him to go jump in the Tiber. Sarina was devastated, but she'd also realized that Jillian had saved her from making a horrible mistake and a complete fool of herself.

That had been the beginning of a beautiful friendship and was the reason Sarina knew that if Jillian had had serious doubts about Rance, she would have voiced them. Further, she would never have agreed to be Sarina's maid of honor if she had thought the marriage was a mistake.

Which, of course, it wasn't, Sarina assured herself as she emerged from the tub at last. "Rance and I have everything," she said, vigorously blotting her skin with plush terry. "Successful careers..." Reaching for the bottle of moisturizer atop the marble vanity, she lavished palmsful on her pores. For some reason she didn't stop to ponder, she pictured the gleaming beaches of Aruba, where Rance had proposed and where, after catching a flight in the morning, they would honeymoon. "A weekend retreat in the Hamptons, season tickets for the Met." She lifted her negligée from the tufted vanity chair. "I'm sure I'll figure out a way to stay awake through an entire opera, eventually."

She slipped the gown over her head. As it cascaded down her torso and limbs, she delighted in the fact that it was little more than an illusion, a confection so light, sheer and delicate, it was like moonglow on those tropical beaches she'd been envisioning since slathering on her moisturizer. Surely, her conjurings must mean she was eager to begin their honeymoon, eager for married life.

"Of course you're eager to begin married life with

Rance," she said as she brushed her red-gold hair into an alluring tousle. "Would Sarina Mann have taken so important a step unless she was absolutely certain?" Putting down the brush, she wiggled her arms into the sleeves of the lace coat that matched her gown and, pleased with her reflection, walked confidently to the door.

But as she reached for the gold knob something made her pause.

Sarina? You know who I am, don't you?

Sarina pursed her lips with annoyance. "Yes. My inner adult. Now go away."

Come on, Sarina. Why don't you just admit there are things about Rance that bother you?

Sarina stepped back. "Nobody's perfect."

Item: You accepted Rance's invitation to observe a face-lift even though you knew you would lose your lunch—

"And did."

Yet, he found an excuse not to attend your office Christmas party. He's never even been to your office.

Sarina shrugged. "Can he help it if he's in such demand that he's always either in surgery or consultation?"

What about that ski trip to Lake Placid you planned and he agreed to take on his weekend off? Convenient, how his back went out.

"He was probably too embarrassed to admit he doesn't know how to ski." Folding her arms, Sarina leaned against the door. "You know how men are."

Okay, let's try this one. He switches your favorite classic-movie station to the Discovery Channel without asking.

"Well…" Walking away from the door, one hand propped on her waist, Sarina scratched her head in thought. "I've got it," she said, snapping her fingers. "He's been a bachelor for so long that—"

What? He figures the woman sitting next to him on the sofa must be a figment of his imagination? Maybe that's why he took you to the Tavern on the Green for your birth-

day when you'd hinted the entire week before that you wanted to go to Le Cirque. He thought he was just hearing voices, right?

Sarina batted her hand at the notion. "He explained that. He said the essence of romance was doing the unexpected."

Translation: After you'd invited the CEO of Global Century, whose job you're in line for, and the entire board of directors to the wedding, you knew you couldn't back out. At least not without looking like a dithering idiot who can't run her own life much less a multinational corporation.

Sarina's shoulders sagged. "Guilty."

And then there's that little matter of the Hex.

As though struck, Sarina inhaled sharply. One brow arched as she brought herself to her full height. "I haven't the least idea what you're talking about."

The hell you don't. You know very well that you were determined the Hex wasn't going to ruin your wedding day, at least not with your help.

"Don't be ridiculous," Sarina said. "I'm too intelligent to believe in hexes." She cocked her head, listening, but no rebuttal sounded in her inner ear. Smiling, she dusted off her hands and started for the door.

So, if you're such a genius, why was your first thought when Rance phoned this morning that the Hex had made him decide to call off the wedding?

Sarina lurched to a halt. "You know why."

Just because your great-grandfather fell down a manhole on the way to his wedding?

"That's one reason. Want another? My grandmother was stung by a swarm of bees on the way to hers. I saw the photographs. Her face looked like a giant pomegranate. And ta-da, the army somehow lost father's request for a two-week leave to get married."

Still, he made the wedding.

"Yes, and spent his honeymoon under lock and key,

awaiting court-martial for going AWOL." Taking a deep breath, Sarina sank onto the edge of the tub. For a moment, she heard nothing but blessed silence. Then—

So now you're married.

Sarina stiffened her spine. "Hitched, and without a hitch."

I have to hand it to you, Sarina. You really outsmarted the hobgoblins this time. By marrying a man you had doubts about, you spoiled the fun they would have had ruining your wedding. And who knows? Maybe you even put an end to the Hex once and for all.

"There's no maybe about it. Trust me, I had it all planned," she said. With a toss of her head and a satisfied smile, Sarina marched to the door and threw it open. As she glanced about the luxurious art-nouveau decor, her eyes came to the magnificent bed and the equally magnificent man standing beside it. Her lips parting, she met the deep azure gaze of her groom.

And the wide, green one of her best friend.

"Jillian?" Her eyes popping, Sarina clutched the scalloped edges of her peignoir about her. "What are you doing there?"

"You mean, what am I doing *here,* don't you, Sarina?" Jillian Wilder spoke breathily over her shoulder, the sleeves of her taffeta bridesmaid's dress rustling ominously.

"No, I mean what are you doing *there,*" Sarina said, jiggling a pointed finger at the short brunette. "In my husband's arms?"

Locked in an embrace, Rance and Jillian gazed at each other, then at Sarina. "My dearest," Rance began, releasing Jillian. "We need to talk."

"Talk?" Scrunching her shoulders, Sarina spread her hands palms up. "Rance, this is our wedding night. We have the rest of our lives to talk."

Pinching the bridge of his nose, Rance Dokter turned

from the woman at his side. "You tell her, Pumpkin. I haven't the heart."

"My poor darling," Jillian said, cupping Rance's shoulder and pressing her cheek to his back.

"Pumpkin? Poor darling?" Sarina charged forward, pried Jillian off her husband and yanked him toward her. "What's going on here, Rance?"

His only answer was a look drowning in guilt.

Sarina stared into his eyes, wondering why they reflected such pain when she was the one with the knife in her back. "How...how could you?"

Jillian stepped between the newlyweds. "I know how you must feel. I know how I would feel in your place. My only hope is that we can all be adult about this." She took Sarina by the shoulders. "Do you think you can do that?"

"Don't...touch me." Sarina jerked from Jillian's entreating grasp. Over her shoulder, she cast Rance a withering stare. "Do you have any idea what I spent on this peignoir? Six hundred big ones."

"Oh, Sarina," Jillian said, clapping her hand on her heart. "You *didn't*."

Straightening, Sarina faced Jillian. "Oh, but *Pumpkin*, I did. What is it to you?"

"Well, not that it isn't scrumptious," Jillian began, her gaze traveling the length of the peignoir. "But I saw it at that little boutique on Lexington Avenue I told you about for three-seventy-five."

Thrusting one foot out, Sarina crossed her arms. "Did not."

Jillian entwined *her* arms. "Did too."

Propping her hands on her waist, elbows akimbo, Sarina advanced on the other woman. "You saw a cheap copy and you know it. For some ridiculous reason, you've always tried to make me feel as though I've paid too much for everything and until now, I've always forgiven you. You're my best friend." She shot a look of disgust at Rance. "You *were* my best friend,'' she said to Jillian. Then, raising her fist, ''So take it back!''

''That's a great idea, Sarina,'' Jillian said. ''Maybe you could return *this* peignoir and buy the cheaper one at—''

''Don't aggravate her, Pumpkin,'' Rance said, backing Jillian away from Sarina.

''It's just that I hate to see her out two hundred and twenty-five dollars,'' Jillian told Rance in a loud whisper. Then, peering past him, she called out to his bride. ''I've never had anything but your best interests at heart, Sarina. I know how careful you always are not to get taken advantage of.''

''Apparently not careful enough.'' Sarina slashed her gaze to her husband, whose sculpted features suddenly seemed fashioned from Silly Putty. ''At least not in your case, Rance. Wouldn't you agree?''

Rance Dokter spun away from both women, raking his hands through sleek, black hair, then faced Sarina. ''You don't plan these things, Sarina,'' he cried, his voice cracking. ''They just happen!''

Her head bobbing, Sarina snorted. ''Even now, you can't help showing contempt for all I hold sacred. That's exactly what Deborah Kerr said in *An Affair to Remember,* just before she dumped the man who gave her the best years of his life!''

''Sarina,'' Rance began, looking askance at her and pointing a remonstrative finger. ''I finally watched that movie with you and I distinctly heard you say you understood how bad she must have felt, but that she couldn't help it. Besides, we haven't known each other long enough for you to give me even a year of your life.''

Sarina's eyes narrowed to gashes. ''But long enough for you to seduce my best friend.''

Jillian thrust her body-by-Rubens—another well-regarded plastic surgeon—in front of Rance. ''He didn't seduce me, Sarina. If anything, I pursued him.''

"*You* pur—" Sarina's arms fell to her sides. "But you wouldn't. You couldn't. Remember Giorgio?"

Jillian's features grew pinched with guilt. Her lips quirked in a plea for mercy. "There's a first time for everything?"

Sarina swayed. Stripped of her every illusion about true friendship, she wanted to make Jillian pay for her wrenching loss of faith. Slowly and menacingly, she started toward the woman who had betrayed her. "Oh, really? Well, it just so happens that I've never strangled anyone before."

Erecting a shield with her outstretched arms, Jillian backed away. "Don't come any closer, Sarina. You're not in your right mind."

"Exactly," Sarina replied, still advancing. "No jury would convict me."

Grabbing Jillian by the shoulders, Rance maneuvered her behind him. "Sarina, I can't let Jillian take all the blame for this. The truth is, it was simply bigger than the both of us."

Sarina gaped at Rance, her eyes smarting. "Don't you even think enough of me to come up with a more original excuse than that?" Shoving past the couple, she paced a circle around a marble-topped table on which sat a crystal vase filled with flowers. "I simply don't understand this," she said, massaging her temples. After a moment, she paused and regarded the two people she'd thought she knew best in the world. The two she'd trusted most. Suddenly, they looked as if they'd stepped from the bar scene in *Star Wars*. "You two always behaved as though you could barely stand to be in the same room."

"I know it seemed that way," Rance said. "But we were really fighting this mad, incredible passion we have for each other. Out of loyalty to you, dear."

Sarina pulled up. "Tell it to the Boy Scouts. I'm fresh out of merit badges." She resumed pacing, then leaned across the table, her fingertips pressed to the cold marble.

"So tell me, how long have you two known each other? In the biblical sense, that is. I mean, when did you decide the hell with loyalty to Sarina, last one to find the condoms is a dirty bird?"

"Oh, Sarina." Her eyes filled with horror, Jillian clutched her throat. She stepped to the table, facing Sarina across it. "Rance and I would never— Not behind your back!"

"And not when I was in the tub, either," Sarina replied, rounding on Jillian. "What do you take me for? You two *must* have consummated this grand passion of yours before today, or else—" Her gaze cut to Rance, standing behind Jillian. "You wouldn't have tried to talk me out of marrying you this morning. That *was* what you were trying to do, wasn't it, Rance?"

"*No,* Sarina. I swear." Hanging his head, he cupped Jillian's shoulders. "Well, perhaps, but only on a subconscious level. Jillian and I never even admitted our feelings for each other until tonight, when we danced at the reception."

"Don't tell me which number. The Hustle, right?" Sarina beseeched the ceiling. "Didn't I say they should shoot the guy who revived disco?" Dragging her fingers over the tabletop, she stalked toward the couple. "But in his absence, one of you will do."

"Violence never solves anything, Sarina," Jillian said, backing into Rance.

"Sarina, don't!" Rance called out as she feigned a lunge toward Jillian.

"Don't what? Don't get upset over my husband and my best friend betraying me on my *wedding night?*" Sarina fought to control the quiver in her chin. "Of all people, you two knew what ruining this occasion would mean to me."

"*Please,* Sarina," Jillian pleaded. "Not the Hex *again.*"

"You're talking sheer nonsense, Sarina," Rance added.

"The notion that there's a curse on your family's weddings, or on any of the other special occasions in your life, is preposterous."

Sarina studied him for a moment, realizing he possessed all the compassion of a hollowed-out tree. "You know what I think is preposterous, Doctor Dokter? Having to explain that you don't have a speech impediment every time you introduce yourself. I should have known you'd turn out to be a dirty, two-timing, belly-crawling double-crosser!" She lifted the vase of cut flowers from the nearby table. "And as for you, Jillian Wilder, do you really believe the reason I never wear that pin you gave me two Christmases ago is that I'm afraid of losing it?" She tipped the vase, poised to hurl its contents.

"You *are* losing it, Sarina!" Jillian held her hands in front of her face. "And I'm sorry you didn't care for that pin," she added, peering through splayed fingers. "I always thought you liked unusual jewelry."

"Unusual, yes. A rendering of a four-topping pizza with one slice missing? Uh-uh." Sarina drew the vase farther back. Jillian lunged for it, but Sarina snatched it from her grasp, holding it above her own head.

"For your own good, Sarina, I beg you not to do something you're only going to regret," Jillian said, keeping her sights fixed on the vase.

Lowering the object, Sarina tucked it under one arm and leveled a thoughtful gaze at her former friend. "You know, Jillian, maybe you're right," she said, her voice turning dulcet, like Julie Andrews' in *The Sound of Music.* "I really must consider that if I throw this vase of water on you, you'll melt and I'll be besieged by a throng of grateful monkeys dressed like bellhops who want to make me their queen." Taking a step to her right, Sarina half turned away. "On the other hand," she added, suddenly turning back. "As John Wayne said, 'The *hell* I won't!'"

"No, Sarina!" Rance rushed to stop her.

Too late. He and Jillian gasped as two quarts of cold water, several day lilies and a bunch of delphiniums and narcissus smacked them in their stunned faces.

Stalking to the door, Sarina yanked it open. "Get out! Both of you!" She pointed to the corridor.

One in front of the other, Rance and Jillian staggered to the door. "I'm truly sorry our friendship had to end like this," Jillian said, pausing.

Sarina was, too. Genuinely sorry it had to end at all. But it wasn't her doing. "You should have thought of that before you danced away with my husband."

Shuffling behind Jillian as she exited the room, Rance gave Sarina a look so guilty, so pained, she felt an involuntary tug at her heart. "I guess there's nothing left to say—except I hope, in time, you'll find it in your heart to forgive me. To forgive us both."

Swallowing a wad of emotions—mostly rage tangled with humiliation and surprisingly, grief—Sarina slowly began to close the door. Was it really possible she could ever forgive them?

"There *is* just one other thing," Rance said, poking his head back inside. He glanced down at the rings on Sarina's finger, the rings whose value, he had once said, were but a poor representation of his devotion.

"Yes, Rance?" she said, softly.

He pointed to the rings. "Are you going to keep those?"

Sarina's jaw dropped. "Oh!" Clamping her hand over the crown of his lowered head, she pushed him into the hall. Furiously, she tugged the three-carat solitaire engagement ring and matching band of baguettes from her finger. "*Forgive* you?" she shouted, stepping into the corridor. "I want to forget I ever *knew* the both of you!" Aiming, she struck each of them with a ring. "Furthermore, if you know what's good for you, you'll be on the next stage out of town!"

Lifting her chin high, Sarina slammed the door and

locked it. Pressing her back to it, she surveyed the damage, including that to her heart, and for the first time that evening, she began to tremble. However imperfect her love for Rance and Jillian had been, she had made commitments to them both, and had honored those commitments. She believed in honoring commitments. If only they had declared their feelings for each other yesterday, she *would* have forgiven them eventually, maybe. But to wait until her wedding night, until vows had been spoken...it was inexcusable.

It was the Hex.

Staggering to the center of the room, she stooped to pick up a yellow daylily. She cupped it in her palm, its fragile petals caressing her skin with their silken vulnerability. She was sorry she had flung it about. Abused it. What had it done to her?

And what had she done to them, Rance and Jillian? When would the Mann Hex end?

Rising, Sarina removed the empty vase from the table and shuffled to the bathroom. After filling the vase in the tub, she gently placed the daylily inside it and set it on the vanity. The longer she stared at the drooping bloom, the more she saw her own heart—battered and alone. Cursed.

Bracing herself, she slapped her palm against the cold marble. "I won't let the Rances and Jillians of this world *or* the Hex destroy me. *I won't!* But I won't give them another shot at me, either. I'm through with friendship and througher than through with love."

After making her vow, Sarina slowly lifted her head and looked in the mirror. Seeing her image blur in a glaze of pooling tears, she stood erect. "And I won't cry." She raised one clenched fist to the heavens.

"As God is my witness, I'll never cry again!"

1

HER CHIN POISED on the tips of her index fingers, psychotherapist Dr. Julia Barrett Brown swiveled toward her new patient. "Sarina, from what you've just told me, I gather that what would have been your first wedding anniversary isn't far off. How do you feel about that?"

Sarina uncrossed her legs and stubbed her unlit microcigarette in the ashtray to her right, breaking the cylinder in two and spilling bits of tobacco. "Cursed as ever, Doctor. How do you feel about it?"

"You'll soon learn that how I feel doesn't matter," Dr. Barrett Brown replied, her lips forming a polite, if impersonal smile. Taking a sudden breath, she tucked in her chin and peered at Sarina above half lenses. "You're undoubtedly an intelligent woman, Sarina, and as a successful business executive, you deal in hard facts. Surely in the light of reason, you can see that the events on your wedding night, while unfortunate, were not the result of an evil spell on your family."

Her hands gripping the arms of the massive, deeply grained and seemingly bottomless leather chair, Sarina peered at Dr. Barrett Brown over the tops of her knees. She felt like a calf in the womb. Having noted that the only photograph on Julia Barrett Brown's desk was of her husband, who shrunk heads across the hall, Sarina speculated that the buttoned-up, late-thirtyish therapist harbored repressed maternal urges she subconsciously vented through her decor. How she'd love a peek at the clinical-looking

Dr. Henley Brown's office, she thought. She'd bet there was an obelisk or two standing around. One thing, however, was certain. His wife didn't know a hex from a hex nut.

"In the light of reason, Doctor, I agree with you," Sarina said. "But there's evidence of the curse in my photo albums going back a hundred years. On his wedding picture, across the sling on his right arm, Great-Grandfather Mann wrote, 'It was that witch, Morgana.'"

Dr. Barrett Brown's mouth twisted with amusement. "Are you sure Great-Grandfather wrote a *w* and not a *b*?"

"Oh, yeah. Morgana ran her coven back in Bavaria," Sarina replied. "She followed Great-Grandfather to America, but when he married Great-Grandmother instead of her, she put a curse on his wedding and the weddings of his descendants. When I was born, though, the Mann Family Curse expanded its coverage. Nearly every special occasion in my life has been a disaster."

Her amusement appearing to have vanished, Dr. Barrett Brown meshed her short, stubby fingers. "I'm sure that if we take a hard, objective look at your assertion, we'll find there's really nothing to it."

"In other words," Sarina began, drawing another cigarette from a slender silver case on the table beside her. "It's all in my head?"

Dr. Barrett Brown smiled again. "I wouldn't be surprised."

"I would," Sarina replied as she tried to balance the cigarette on the tip of her index finger. "I could have sworn it was in the dining room."

The therapist blinked. "Excuse me?"

Sarina's gaze followed the tottering cigarette. "That's where my parents told me, the Christmas I was nine, that they were splitting up."

Frowning, the therapist rubbed the heels of her hands together. "Insensitive of your parents, certainly. But—" She swirled one hand in the hair. "Cosmic mischief? I

don't think so, Sarina. You were young and probably unaware that your parents' marriage had been in trouble for
some time.''

The doctor was undoubtedly right about that. But, then,
how would she explain Tuffy? "I had a cocker spaniel
when I was a kid," she said, flipping the cigarette in the
air then catching it in cupped hands. "On my twelfth birthday he was hit by a car.''

A cloud scudded across Dr. Barrett Brown's features,
casting a shadow of doubt over her face. Soon, however,
she regained her expression of calm detachment. "Well
now, the fact that, aside from your wedding, two traumatic
episodes in your life just happened to occur on two separate, special occasions isn't exactly conclusive proof of a
curse, is it?''

Determining that she had her work educating Julia Barrett Brown cut out for her, Sarina kicked her shoes off and
curled her legs on the wide, plush seat. "I missed my high-
school graduation," she said, then slanted her gaze at the
doctor. "Chicken pox.''

"I see." Craning her neck, Dr. Barrett Brown began to
scratch. She trailed her short nails from beneath her chin,
across her throat, around to her nape, and finally, delved
inside the back of her jacket. Catching sight of the elbow
crooked in front of her nose, she abruptly unwound, cleared
her throat, and lifted her pen in the air. "Nevertheless—''

"I had been named valedictorian, too." Sarina wondered
if she was perhaps being cruel. After all, it was probably
the doctor's first time treating a patient with a hex and
Sarina really ought to be gentle with her. On the other hand,
did she have a choice? She couldn't have the therapist
thinking she was crazy. "Cynthia Zimmer—who virtually
guaranteed that no boy in my class would ever notice I
have blue eyes and dark red hair when she started the rumor
that I wore falsies—took my place.''

Dr. Barrett Brown's mouth formed a soundless O, then

she rolled her eyes, tossed her hand, and gave an embarassed laugh. "High school," she said cajolingly.

Sarina didn't laugh. "She got her picture taken with the governor."

The therapist's right brow arched.

"And a summer internship in his office."

Dr. Barrett Brown's head jerked to one side.

"She married his son."

Julia Barrett Brown sucked in her lips.

"Today she's the ambassador to a small, independent island state where there's no poverty, no crime, no taxes, and it rains only between ten at night and two in the morning."

Dr. Julia Barrett Brown clawed the left side of her face, her little finger snagging her lower lip and holding it inside out. Her eyes were dull, zombielike, as she stared at Sarina, who was beginning to experience a strange mix of guilt and concern.

"Doctor? Are you all right?"

Julia Barrett Brown searched for her voice and failed on the first attempt. "Yes," she said, barely above a whisper. "I'm quite all right." Rising, she tugged the creases from her sedate jacket. "Sarina," she began, waving her pen, "I can well understand how you might be tempted to wonder if you would be living in paradise now if it hadn't been for the chicken pox. On the other hand, as a scientist, I simply cannot allow you to persist in this belief in a curse. Cynthia Zimmer merely happened to be in the right place at the right time."

"Oh, and I definitely believe in that phenomenon, Doctor." Sarina sat up, exuding earnestness. "It even happened to me once."

Beaming, Dr. Barrett Brown breathed a sigh of relief. "There, you see? We all have our share of good luck as well as bad."

"No doubt about it," Sarina said. "You don't have to

tell me how fortunate I was that when my apartment building was struck by lightning, I was at work, being promoted to vice president.''

Clutching her throat, Dr. Barrett Brown gulped. "You don't say?"

"I was even luckier than that." Sarina broke the cigarette in two and deposited the halves in the ashtray. "Just the day before, I had increased my contents insurance, so even though the fire destroyed nearly everything I owned, it was all covered."

Julia Barrett Brown slumped into her chair. Her chin quivering and her eyes puddling with tears, she lowered her forehead to her hand.

Sarina felt like a monster. "Oh, don't cry, please," she said, birthing herself from the mother of all chairs. She rushed to the silently sobbing woman and hugged her wracking shoulders. "There, there. I'm fine, really. I'm used to it." Plucking a tissue from the box on the doctor's desk, she thrust it under her nose. "Here, blow."

After Dr. Barrett Brown did as she'd been instructed, she gazed tearfully up at her patient. "I'm sorry, Sarina. I've never lost control like this before. I don't know what came over me."

"Don't feel bad, Doc. It's early, and if I had to start every day listening to other people's problems, I'd cry, too." Sarina walked to the table beside the leather chair, removing yet another floral-tipped cigarette from the silver case. "If I *could* cry."

Wiping her tearstained glasses, Dr. Barrett Brown paused and gazed at Sarina from beneath shirred brows. "What do you mean, if you *could* cry?"

Wrapping her arms around herself, Sarina turned. Instantly, she caught sight of a print hanging on the wall opposite her and, intrigued, started toward it. "You know that scene at the end of *Love is a Many-Splendored Thing*, when William Holden gets killed in Korea and Jennifer

Jones keeps thinking she sees him on that high and windy hill?''

"I've never seen that movie.''

"Let me put it this way,'' Sarina said, stepping up to the print and examining it closely. "Up until my wedding day, I couldn't watch that scene without having to go on a glucose IV afterward. I'm talking severe dehydration.'' Looking over her shoulder at the doctor, she shrugged. "But now, I don't even mist over. No sniffle. No knot in the throat, no—''

"Sarina, are you telling me you haven't cried since your wedding day?'' Alarm flashed in Dr. Barrett Brown's eyes.

Sarina turned fully toward the therapist. "You got it.''

Dr. Barrett Brown slowly rose, folded her arms and started toward Sarina. "But you did have a good cry over the betrayal and loss of Rance and Jillian, didn't you?''

"And give Morgana the satisfaction? Uh-uh.'' Sarina failed to mention that for a month following that night, she'd done everything from pressing her eyeballs with the heels of her hands to nearly biting off the tip of her tongue to keep from crying.

"In the last ten months,'' Dr. Barrett Brown began, both amazement and concern in her gaze, "hasn't anything brought tears to your eyes?''

Sarina looked askance, as though searching her memory. "I stubbed my toe on the corner of my dresser once, but otherwise, nothing.''

Julia Barrett Brown replaced her glasses and lifting her chin, regarded Sarina through the lenses. "But other behavior has taken the place of crying, hasn't it?''

Sarina didn't like the doctor's cryptic tone—her entire demeanor, which had gone from motherly to Mother Superior. She felt as though she'd been caught in the act, only she didn't know what the act was. "Please, if I had wanted to play guessing games I'd have called my stockbroker.''

Dr. Barrett Brown lowered her eyes to the white cylinder

between Sarina's fingers, then removed her glasses and looked directly into Sarina's eyes. "I'll give it to you straight, then. It's obvious to me that your inability to effect a truly cathartic experience has resulted in the sublimation of your trauma as evidenced by the adoption of compensatory behavior."

Folding her arms, Sarina slowly fell to one side, her shoulder bumping against the wall beside the watercolor print. "If that's straight, so's the tax code."

Smiling, Julia Barrett Brown batted her eyelashes prodigiously. "It's really quite simple," she said. "Instead of crying over what happened on your wedding night, you've taken to brandishing cigarettes you admit you never light, much less smoke. Now why do you suppose you substituted that particular behavior?"

Cupping her chin, Sarina looked at the doctor. "I have a death wish, but I'm too chicken to carry it out?"

Dr. Barrett Brown fixed an intent gaze on her patient. "No, Sarina. You're afraid of relationships."

Sarina shot off the wall. "I'm not the fearful type, but even if I were, I don't see how you could deduce that from this." Grasping it at one end, she thrust the cigarette at the therapist.

Dr. Barrett Brown shook her head pityingly. "You've just made my point. In our culture the cigarette is a symbol of all that is socially and politically incorrect. You wield yours as a warning to others not to get too close." She pushed her glasses to the top of her head. "You have very deep-seated hostilities, my dear."

Brows arched, Sarina raised the cigarette to eye level. After giving it a full rotation, she still saw nothing other than a white paper roll containing a dose of dried, crushed, shredded leaves. As she stubbed it in the ashtray on the table beneath the print, she peered up at the therapist. "Look, I used to be a two-pack-a-day smoker, and when

I'm under a lot of stress, I revert to carrying around cigarettes. Besides, I can't fit my blanky in my purse.''

Shaking her head, Dr. Barrett Brown nevertheless smiled. ''Sarina, you're in denial.''

''Forgive me, Doctor,'' Sarina said as she returned to the leather chair and put on her shoes. ''I'll admit that everything I know about psychology I learned from watching Alfred Hitchcock movies. But I think you're the one who's in denial.''

Covering her heart with her hand, Dr. Barrett Brown gasped. ''I beg your pardon.''

Straightening, Sarina folded her arms. ''Do you mind if I ask you a personal question?''

''If it will help you to trust me, Sarina.''

''I've kind of been off trust, lately,'' Sarina replied. ''But I can't help wondering if you and Dr. Brown have children.''

Julia Barrett Brown's expression passed from surprised to sad to surly. ''My husband and I feel that we couldn't give both a family and our practice the attention each deserves. In a sense, our patients are our family.''

''That's what I thought.'' Sarina returned to the print on the wall, motioning for the doctor to join her. ''I hate to get Freudian without a license, but this looks exactly like a gynecological X-ray. See,'' she said, swirling her hand over the print. ''There's the uterus, ovaries, fallopian tubes.''

Lowering her glasses from the top of her head, Dr. Barrett Brown stooped to examine the print. Abruptly, she shot up, turned and walked back to her desk. ''I believe we were discussing your aversion to personal involvements.''

''*You* were discussing. I was denying, remember?'' Sarina took her black cashmere topcoat and Italian leather shoulder bag from the coatrack. ''Look,'' she said, stuffing her cigarette case in her bag. ''The reason I don't cry is because I don't want to. I won't give Morgana even more reason to keep the Mann Family Hex going. My only problem is that I've been having trouble sleeping lately. If you don't think you can help me, perhaps I should just leave now." Folding her coat over her arm, she headed to the door.

"You're free to do as you like, of course." Dr. Barrett Brown picked up her pad and pen. "But you still have ten minutes, so why don't you tell me more about your insomnia?" Unlike before, her tone was soft, personal, genuinely caring.

Sarina felt sorry for childless Julia Brown, and bad for having all but accused her of incompetence. "I—I—I don't know," she said uncertainly. Then, "Can I sleep on it?"

Pursing a smile, the therapist laced her fingers and looked warmly at Sarina. "I'd like to help you, if you'll allow me."

Why not? Sarina thought. After all, her physician had recommended she see Dr. Barrett Brown, and if she didn't get some sleep soon, finding the energy to keep up with the demands of her job would be the least of her problems. She wouldn't have a job. Sighing, she returned to the womblike chair and, lacking the strength to endure another birthing, perched on the arm. "What do you suggest?"

"I could medicate you," the doctor replied. "But that would only be masking the root cause of your insomnia. In other words, your loneliness."

Sarina watched as the therapist rose and walked past her, following an indirect path to the print on the wall. "But...I'm not lonely. If anything, there are too many people in my life. I have a large staff to manage, and scores of business associates around the world, and—"

"But no one person you're close to." Julia Brown studied the print from a variety of angles, then shaking her head, as if bewildered, looked at Sarina. "Believe me, I can understand why you've sworn off both romance and friendship, but hiding behind your job isn't the answer."

How many times had Sarina given herself the same caution? And always, her response had been the same. "It beats getting your heart trampled." Rising, she walked toward the doctor. "Besides, things are going just fine and I don't want to tempt fate. I have an exciting job that takes me to the capitals of the world. I have a beautiful apartment in the East Sixties. I'm financially independent and can look forward to a wonderful retirement—"

"Alone."

Sarina paused, sliding her jaw to one side. "I *like* it that way."

"Sarina, everyone needs someone to talk to, someone they can entrust their most intimate feelings to."

Sarina gazed around the expensively, if weirdly, decorated office. "Isn't that what I'm paying you a usurious rate for?"

"As good a therapist as I like to think I am," Dr. Barrett Brown said, "I can't take the place of a friend. And that's exactly what you need, a new best friend."

"I don't have time to socialize," Sarina replied. "Anyway, I don't need to. I'm on very friendly terms with the women in my office."

"That isn't the same as being friends with those women, Sarina. As your subordinates, they can't afford your friendship. They can't be completely honest with you, the way a true friend would."

"You mean they won't tell me when I have toilet paper stuck to my shoe?"

"Something like that," the doctor replied.

Shrugging into her coat, Sarina said, "I'm sure you're mistaken, Doctor. They're very loyal, if not to me personally, to the company. They know I represent Global Century and they wouldn't let me project anything less than the best image."

"Maybe so," Dr. Barrett Brown replied, sounding unconvinced. "But if I had to guess, I'd say they never ask you to go to a movie or shopping after work."

The last time Sarina had gone shopping with a friend was when she and Jillian had combed Madison Avenue, searching for the perfect wedding dress. In truth, she'd done precious little shopping at all in recent months. Bargain hunting wasn't much fun unless there was someone to witness the kill. "No," she admitted, "but my accountant is a lot happier. Look, Doc," she said, her gaze following Dr. Barrett Brown as she returned to her desk and began flipping through her Rolodex. "I don't need a man and I don't need a bosom buddy. All I need is a good night's sleep, so can't you just give me something to help me—"

"Take this," the therapist said, handing her the piece of paper on which she'd been scribbling.

Sarina read it, then gave a puzzled look. "This isn't a prescription."

"No, it's the name and phone number of an agency I think can provide what you need while you're working on regaining your trust in people."

"What I need is somebody to play backgammon with at three in the morning. Do they provide that?"

Dr. Barrett Brown crooked a finger over a tiny smile. "I doubt it, but you can always ask."

Sarina read the name on the slip of paper. "Friends in High Places? These people aren't from Arkansas, are they?"

With a chuckle and a glance at her watch, Julia Brown ushered Sarina to the door. "Friends in High Places is an agency right here in town that provides professional companions for people at the top, where as the saying goes, it's lonely. I know the owners personally and I believe they'll do an excellent job of matching you with someone who shares your interests."

Sarina's eyes got wide. "You mean if I feel like playing tennis in the middle of the afternoon, I just call my rent-a-friend?'' She thrust the slip at the doctor. "No thanks, doctor. Things aren't so bad that I have to pay for friendship, and if it ever does come to that, you can bet all the neuroses in Manhattan I won't be calling Friends in High Places. They sound like an excuse for a special prosecutor.''

Dr. Barrett Brown closed her hand around Sarina's and the slip of paper. "Just give it some thought. If you decide you're not interested, that's fine.'' She opened the door. "Same time next week?''

Sarina hesitated. Did she really want to open doors, locked doors, to places inside her she'd just as soon remained in the dark? On the other hand, she needed to sleep. Over-the-counter remedies weren't working, and deep down, she was as reluctant to take prescription pills as the therapist was to prescribe them. "Next week,'' she said. As she turned to leave, she glanced once more at the print on the far wall. "But Julia, if I were you, I'd have a talk with Dr. Brown tonight. *After* I'd stopped at Victoria's Secret on my way home tonight and picked up a little something. A *very* little something.''

On her way to the elevators, Sarina took another look at the information Dr. Barrett Brown had given her. Friends in High Places, indeed. She needed a rented friend like she needed another hex, and to prove it, she had some shopping of her own to do before she returned to the office.

MAX EVANGELIST STOOD in the conference room of Friends in High Places, looking out the window at gently falling snow and listening to his New York employees file in. Apparently, his partner and best friend wasn't turning over any new leaves with the new year. As usual, Tony Dario was late for a meeting. At moments like these, Max was certain there had been something besides tobacco in the cigar he'd smoked that night three years ago, the night he'd offered Tony a partnership in his business. The gesture had violated one of his cardinal rules: never enter into a business venture with your best friend, especially if your best friend also happens to be married to your sister. But Max had been smoking the same Macanudos from the same shop near his midtown apartment for years, and other than selling Tony an equal stake in the company, he hadn't done anything more rash than giving some thought to asking Camilla Price to marry him.

Fortunately, the thought had been fleeting and so was Camilla. He wasn't the marrying kind. From what he could tell, marriage was high on demand and low on supply of the basic human needs—money, sex, companionship, and closet space. Unfortunately, he tended to forget that observation every time he came within ten yards of a burnished redhead like Camilla.

His other weakness, he well knew, was his kid sister Micah. After their mother had died and their father, after failing at several businesses, had turned to booze, Max assumed the role of parent. He'd raised Mike, and happily. But why did he now have to bring up her husband, too? Most kids with a paper route had more business sense than Tony had.

True, when Max had asked Tony to come into the agency as an equal partner, he knew Tony's strength was the congeniality he'd capitalized on to become a top salesman. He'd even counted on that strength to complement his own, which was the willingness to make tough, bottom-line decisions. They'd make a classic duo, he'd reasoned, an honest version of Butch Cassidy and the Sundance Kid. Instead, they had both been acting like Vincent Price in some old horror flick from the fifties, barely concealing their growing animosity toward each other beneath ultra-urbane exteriors. Lately, even that thin veneer of civility was beginning to crack.

Just last week, they'd gotten into a verbal scuffle over

whether or not one of the Friends, at his client's request, should have walked the client's dog.

"The Friends are professionals, Tony," Max had argued. "College graduates who are multiversed in finance, the arts, sports, languages, psychology, gourmet foods and fine wines. They shouldn't be asked to add poop-scooping to their résumés."

"I'm not suggesting we become an errand service, Max," Tony had replied. "But I just don't see the harm in the Friends doing an occasional personal favor for their clients."

Perching on one corner of his desk, Max had regarded Tony with a strange mixture of admiration and frustration. Tony was one of the kindest and most decent men he'd ever known. Max wouldn't have let Mike marry the man if he'd been otherwise. But Tony just didn't have the foresight to anticipate the problems his anything-goes attitude toward Friend/client relationships could cause. "The harm is that personal favors eventually lead to personal commitment. Once a Friend becomes emotionally involved with a client, he puts himself and the entire agency at risk."

Tony had laughed. "Risk for what, Max? Fleabites?"

"I wish that was the worst case scenario." Rising, Max had walked to the window behind his desk and gazed south across the whitened skyline, toward his and Tony's old neighborhood. Max had come a long way from the Lower East Side, and not just in terms of the number of blocks closer he was to Park Avenue. He'd enjoyed one successful career and was now in the midst of another. Last year, the agency had been profiled in *Entrepreneur* magazine, which called it an "up-and-comer for the nineties and beyond." At his initiative, it had even started branching out, opening offices in Chicago and L.A. But he wasn't so caught up with increasing his net worth that he'd forgotten about protecting his employees.

"Let me ask you a question," he'd said, facing Tony.

"What do you think is going to happen to the Friends when they can't remain objective about their clients any longer, when they start carrying around their problems, worrying about their divorces and their sick kids? How long do you think it will be before they start feeling guilty about charging for their friendship?"

Tony had shoved his hands in his pockets. "Now I see what's really bothering you. You're afraid they'll start understating their hours and the agency will lose money."

"What I'm afraid of," Max had replied, slapping a hand on his desk, "is losing good people to depression and burnout. Sure, I'm concerned about the agency getting in a bind. Every one of the Friends is too highly skilled to be replaced overnight. But—" Glancing at the group photograph taken at the last company holiday party, he picked it up. After putting names with the faces of each of the Friends, he held the picture out to Tony. "What happens to *them* when they can't work?"

Taking the photograph, Tony gave it serious study. "I agree that burnout is a potential problem," he said. As he set the photo down, a bright smile lit his face. "And I have the solution. We'll provide Friends for the Friends!"

Max had hardly known what to say. He'd just heard the *Harvey* of all harebrained ideas. "And what happens to *those* Friends, Tony? Where will it end?" He released a heavy sigh. "I'm sorry, but we'll have to make it clear to the Friends that if they can't keep from becoming emotionally involved with their clients, they should begin looking for another line of work."

Tony jabbed a finger at Max. "Then *you* tell them, because I can't ask them to do the impossible! If you'd ever been a Friend to a client, you'd know that's exactly what you're asking." Turning, he stalked out the door, slamming it behind him.

And leaving Max dumbstruck. It was true; he'd never been in the field, so to speak. That reminder had led to his calling this morning's meeting. He really did need to hear what the Friends had to say on the subject of personal involvement with their clients. He also had to find a way to spare his sister the pain a permanent breach between her husband and her brother would cause her. That was the last thing Max wanted to put her through, especially now. She was pregnant with his nephew.

"Mr. Evangelist?"

Turning from the window, Max encountered Sylvia Weinstein's uncertain expression, which was multiplied twenty times on the face of the others sitting at the conference table. "Yes, Sylvia?"

"We're all here, except for Tony."

She'd called him "Tony," Max noted. Around the office, *he* was "Mr. Evangelist," but Tony was Mr. Nice Guy, even when he kept everyone waiting. Twelve minutes this time, he saw, checking his watch. As far as he was concerned, unless Mr. Nice Guy was being held hostage by terrorists, he had no excuse for wasting the Friends' time. They had a job to do. At least that was what Max intended to impress on them this morning, in hopes of dispelling Tony's notion that they were engaged in social work. But if Tony didn't care to accept Max's invitation to defend his views, so be it.

"Let's get started, people," he said, taking his place at one end of the table. "As you all know, the idea for Friends in High Places grew out of my observations of corporate life. But I think you all need to hear the story in more detail."

Max recounted his experience working in a multinational real-estate conglomerate. He'd observed executives on the rise and saw that each time they were promoted to offices higher in the corporate tower, they became more isolated, socially and professionally. The fast track, they discovered, is booby-trapped with resentment, jealousy, competitiveness, even fear. Although they had acquired power, prestige and money, they could no longer play a round of golf without having to play corporate politics, or have an unguarded conversation with someone who stood neither to gain nor lose from the encounter. Someone they could trust.

"Loneliness," Max said, "is too frequently the price of achievement."

What he didn't say was that he'd more than observed this phenomenon. He'd lived it. The more successful he'd become, the fewer people he could count as friends. Even his longtime friends—except for Tony, to his credit—gradually stopped calling to ask him to meet for a beer or to join them for softball in the park. Not that he was blameless. Too often he'd had to beg off. He'd had a plane to catch or a client to wine and dine. In any event, people change; their worlds and their interests inevitably drift apart. By the time Max realized what had happened, he was very nearly an island.

But having seen how his father's relentless self-pity had served no purpose other than to defeat him in business and in life, Max had decided to turn his problem into an opportunity. He didn't relate this to the Friends, of course. He merely stated that his observations had convinced him of the need for an agency that would provide discreet and professional companionship for clients at the pinnacles of their busy and demanding careers. Among them, corporate leaders, diplomats, dignitaries.

"Just last week," he said with a touch to each of his gold cufflinks, "we placed a Friend with a United Nations delegate. And if we're to continue to enjoy such prestige, we have to root out the unprofessionalism that's begun to creep—"

"Sorry, I'm late everybody," Tony said, entering the room. Only his jeans-clad legs and loafers were visible beneath the huge white ceramic pot he was holding. Tied with a pink ribbon, it sprouted a tall and gangly schefflera covered in plastic. "I had quite a time getting this out of the cab. Come to think of it, getting it in wasn't exactly a breeze, either.'' Reaching his place at the end of the table opposite Max, he set the plant down, turning it several times until he was satisfied with its position. Then he took his seat.

His elbows propped on the arms of his chair, Max stared at Tony above clasped hands. ''Are you both quite comfortable?''

The Friends looked from Max to Tony.

Grinning, Tony gave Max two thumbs up.

The Friends turned to Max.

''You can't know how that makes my day,'' he said, sitting forward and picking up the pen in front of him. ''There's just one small matter you might be able to clear up for me.''

''Shoot,'' Tony said.

Don't tempt me, Max thought. ''I understand your being over fifteen minutes late, *again,* because you had a hard time getting that dandy bit of flora both in and out of the cab. What I don't quite get is why you felt compelled to bring it here in the first place.'' He gazed questioningly at the Friends. ''If it's Take Your Houseplant to Work Week, one of you should have told me.''

Twenty pairs of eyes looked at the schefflera.

''You know, that's not a bad idea, Max,'' Tony said, reaching forward and pouring coffee into a cup. Next, he opened two packets of sugar and a packet of creamer and poured them into the coffee. Then, taking a spoon from the tray, he swirled it around the steaming brew, sipped, emptied another packet of sugar into the cup, and swirled again.

Leaning to one side, Max tapped the pen in the palm of his hand. ''Sweet enough for you?'' he asked, giving Tony a saccharine smile. ''Take your time, now. We really have nothing better to do.''

The Friends watched Tony slowly sip his coffee, then send Max a look of satisfaction. ''Perfect.''

They saw Max's eyes narrow to slits. They looked at Tony.

"As you know, Max," he began, taking another gulp. "Our Jodie's been out with a bad case of the flu. I'm taking this plant over to Shady Rest for her."

Max's eyes popped. "Good Lord, I talked to her only a few days ago and she said she was beginning to feel much better."

Tony laughed. "Shady Rest is a nursing home, Max, not a cemetery."

Max's eyes narrowed. "Jodie's in a nursing home?"

Helping himself to a jelly doughnut from the same tray that held the coffee, Tony took a bite. "Not Jodie," he said thickly, littering crumbs onto the tabletop. "Her client's mother. She promised she'd visit the old gal."

"Oh, Tony," Sylvia said. "What a lovely gesture."

Max threw the pen down, sending it skidding past the Friends. "Be that as it may, Sylvia, it's exactly the kind of personal involvement I've been warning 'Tony' about. Such gestures could lead to sticky emotional entanglements we can't begin to predict, much less prevent." Seeing her eyes tear up, Max took a deep, calming breath. "I'm only thinking of your good, Sylvia. Of the good of all the Friends."

"Give her a break, Max," Tony said, fixing an empathetic gaze on the grandmotherly Sylvia, who was blowing her nose.

With their partnership *and* their friendship at stake, Max thought, how could Tony so blatantly and publicly undermine him by agreeing to help Jodie keep a personal promise to a client, then flaunting the fact that he had? This time, he'd gone too far. "The only break I'm considering is of your neck," he said, his tone chillingly detached.

Aghast, the Friends followed the direction of Max's blistering serve.

"Okay, Max. I can see you want to get down to business,

so let's just do it." Tony pushed up the sleeves of his slouch-shouldered sport coat.

Eyes even wider, the Friends gazed after Tony's snappy return.

"It's about time," Max said, scoring and claiming their attention. "I called this meeting because the agency needs one policy covering Friend/client relationships. Obviously, I think my policy strictly forbidding personal involvement should prevail over Mr. Dario's approach, which seems to be based on the collected sayings of Barney. But first, I want to hear your views. I want to know if you think it's possible for you to keep your feelings out of your relationships with your clients. Larry," he said, looking at the man seated to his left, "let's start with you."

"I treat this job as I have every other job I've ever had," Larry replied. "At the end of the day, I leave it at the office."

"Ditto for me," Carol, who sat to Larry's left, said. "When a client starts telling me she's worried her husband is playing around, I change the subject. No job is worth losing sleep over."

"Same."

"Same."

As they went down the line, Max cast several see-I-told-you-so looks at his partner. Then the question came to Sylvia.

The fifty-something woman looked first at Tony, then at Max, then burst into tears. "I think you're all perfectly horrible," she said, blowing her nose again. "When you've had a client for two years and she's suddenly transferred to London, as I just found out my Ms. Caparelli's been, how can you not feel the loss of a—" sniffle "—dear friend? I even used to baby-sit for her—on my own time, of course. And now, who knows if I'll ever see those sweet children again?" Burying her face in her handkerchief, Sylvia stifled sobs.

Tony handed back one of Max's smug looks.

"Oh, can it, Sylvia," Carol said. "You never should have let yourself get that involved to begin with."

"Don't you dare talk to her that way," Jonah fired from across the table. "You're just jealous because Sylvia goes out of her way for her clients and gets twice as many recommendations as the rest of us do. You've never been recommended at all!"

"So, who wants to be recommended for Doormat of the Year?" Carol folded her thick arms across her thicker bosom.

A volley of verbal shots flew across the table. Tony stepped into the cross fire. "Friends, please. I'm sure we can all handle our disagreements in a civilized manner." He repeated his plea several times, to no avail.

Finally, Max rose, and placing his fingers in his mouth, emitted an eardrum-shattering whistle. Instantly, the combatants ceased lobbing word bombs and turned their pop-eyed gazes on him. "Let's proceed, shall we? The question is, do you think it's possible to keep your friendships with your clients strictly business? A simple yes or no will do."

They began with the Friend seated next to Sylvia. "Yes," she said.

"Yes."

"Yes."

"No."

"I'm not sure."

"No."

"Pregnant."

"Yes."

"Whoa," Max said, raising his hand. "What was that?"

"I said yes, Mr. Evangelist," Sam replied.

"No, before that." Max stared at the young woman to Sam's right. Her gaze darted about the room, avoiding Max's. "Zelda? I don't think I quite caught your answer. Would you mind repeating it?"

Bending back the fingers of her left hand one by one, Zelda ventured a look at Max. "Pregnant?"

Max pressed his knuckles into the table. "That's what I thought you said. And may I ask, Zelda, how the news of this blessed event relates to your clients?"

"It's very related to one of my clients, Mr. Evangelist," the brown-haired former anthropology teacher replied. "The baby is Ms. Sheridan's brother's. I met him at a party at her house on Long Island."

Max stretched his neck. "I see." Gazing at the others, he said, "Will you excuse us?" He crooked a finger at Tony.

A moment later, Max and Tony stood toe-to-toe in the outer office. "Are you satisfied now?" Max said, his voice and blood pressure rising. "Didn't I tell you that your touchy-feely policies would lead to something like this?"

"Come off it, Max," Tony shouted back. "People are people. This was bound to happen sooner or later."

Max thumbed his chest. "If I'd had my way months ago and we'd laid down a policy of firing any Friend who so much as mailed a letter for a client, it would have happened a lot later."

Turning away, Tony threw his hands up. "So what do you want to do, Max? Make an example of Zelda?" Looking across his shoulder, he wired Max a challenge. "Are you really heartless enough to deprive a single mother of her job? Because if you are—"

"Oh, I'm not thinking of firing Zelda," Max replied. Circling the reception desk, he trailed his finger across it, then fixed Tony firmly in his sights. "But I do think it's time this agency had one fewer employee."

His gaze wary, Tony folded his arms across his T-shirt. "What are you getting at?"

Max folded his arms across his tie. "Did you see how they were at each other's throats in there a minute ago? *We* did that to them, pal, by sending them conflicting signals about the culture of this agency. They don't know if we're supposed to be a legitimate business or a lonely-hearts club." Turning away, Max rubbed the tension forming above his eyes. As sure as he was of what he was about to propose, he was even more certain he'd never felt worse about anything in his life. "One of us has to go, Tony. If we don't end our partnership, we'll lose our friendship. I'm sure you don't want that any more than I do, if for no other reason than that we both know it would kill Mike."

As Tony turned toward the filing cabinets, Max thought he saw a shimmer in the man's eyes. "I suppose you're right," Tony said, propping his elbow atop one of the cabinets and his cheek on his fist. "Don't worry about me, Max. I'm sure my old firm will take me back."

Max's jaw dropped. "I meant that *I* should leave the agency, not you. You're the family man, not to mention that your family happens to be my sister and nephew."

"No way, Max," Tony said. "You started this business. You should be the one to stay on."

Max shook his head no. "I'd only look like the heavy in Mike's eyes."

Tony shrugged. "Then how *do* we decide?"

The men circled each other in solitary thought.

"I guess we should have signed those buyout agreements a long time ago," Tony said.

"Yeah." Max clamped a hand on Tony's shoulder. "But we were both willing to bet our last dollars that nothing would ever come between us. And now—"

"That's it, Max!" Tony snapped his fingers. "A bet. Whichever one of us wins buys out the other and gets sole ownership of the agency."

Max frowned thoughtfully. Still, he wanted details. "What kind of bet?"

After Tony had thought for a moment, he began excitedly laying out the terms of the wager.

"Let me get this straight," Max said, after Tony had

finished. "If I can prove to you that I can keep from getting emotionally involved with a client for six weeks, then I win. But if I can't—"

"Then the agency is mine," Tony said.

Max looked away, considering. "There's just one thing. How can I prove I have no feelings for my client?"

"You can't," Tony replied. "But I think I know a way to prove that you do. How I do that, of course, will be my secret."

Max pulled at his chin. "You know, for once you've come up with a screwy idea that just might work."

Tony fixed a squint-eyed stare on Max. "Remember, Max, you can't do anything to enlist the client's help, like revealing our bet."

"I won't need the client's help, pal," Max shot back.

"I'll have spies tailing you."

"I hope they can handle boredom," Max replied. "Because they won't have anything to report."

"You're kidding yourself, Max," Tony said, shaking his head. "You may think you can separate your heart from your head, but I know you better than you know yourself. And I'm telling you, you can't do it."

Max smiled broadly. "Just to show you how wrong I think you are, I'll even let you choose the client."

His self-assurance reflected in his own smile, Tony extended his hand. "You've got yourself a bet."

Max clasped Tony's hand, sealing their bargain. "I've got myself an agency."

2

"How do you like it, Liz?" Sarina stood in front of her desk, holding up the shortest, tightest, loudest dress she could find at the one designer boutique that maintained a list of the ten worst-dressed party girls in New York. A collage of hot pinks, oranges, greens and yellows, with enormous, puff sleeves and a bustier-style bodice, the dress also had peekaboo cutouts at the hips and above each pointy, molded, bejeweled breast. Sarina flattened it against her body, over her tailored, navy-blue-striped suit. "I just couldn't resist it," she said, scrutinizing Liz's expression to gauge her reaction to the outlandish outfit. As she had expected, the analytical data manager's mental files appeared to be processing a statement of profound disgust. She knew she could count on no-nonsense Liz Elliot to declare this particular glad rag an item for a GLAD bag. But why should she spoil her own fun by making it too easy for Liz to state the obvious? "I guess I was just in the mood for something a little different."

Liz Elliot's eyebrows shot up and over the frames of her glasses. "Oh, it certainly is that, Ms. Mann."

Sarina frowned. Why was Liz muffling her criticism? Why hadn't she launched into one of her let's-cut-out-the-garbage evaluations and said exactly what her expression showed? Because she's in shock, Sarina thought. She just needs stimulation. "Isn't it fabulous? I mean, have you ever seen anything like it?"

"No, Ms. Mann. I can honestly say I never have."

This isn't working, Sarina thought. She had sworn to Dr. Barrett Brown that the women in her office felt free to be absolutely frank with her, and to prove it, she had devised what she thought was a brilliant means of testing her contention. Perhaps the problem lay in the way she had framed her questions. "You do like it, don't you? I mean, you don't think it's too bright?"

Liz looked at the dress, cocking her head this way and that, considering it from an arc of different angles. "To tell you the truth—"

"Yes?" Sarina stepped closer, barely able to conceal her glee.

"I'm color-blind. Maybe you'd better ask one of the others."

Sarina felt her hopes take a dive into the bustier. Throwing the dress over the back of her chair, she stepped to her phone and asked her administrative assistant to send the other women on her staff into her office. When the twelve had gathered before her, she said, "I called you all in here because I want to ask your opinions about something, woman-to-woman. And don't hold back. I want you to be completely honest."

Lifting the dress from her chair, she held it to her form. "Well?"

Silence.

Vamping to the center of the room, she struck a pose. "Terrific, isn't it?" From the looks on their faces, Sarina thought, they couldn't be more stunned if she'd been standing there naked. One of them was bound to crack. "Well, isn't it?"

Liz nudged Kim MacCauley, Sarina's administrative assistant, in the ribs, appointing her spokeswoman. "It's…incredible, Ms. Mann," Kim said.

"Incredible, incredible."

"Unbelievable."

"Out of this world."

"I can't imagine where you ever found it."

Sarina gaped. She'd never heard so much of what sounded like fawning in her entire life. On the other hand, they were twelve diverse women; they were probably only exhibiting a healthy tolerance for a variety of tastes. Besides, she hadn't given them a serious enough reason— yet—to venture an honest opinion.

"I thought it would be perfect for that big party we're giving for our partners in the Hong Kong project next week."

Sarina watched the women slide furtive glances at one another. She waited for one of them to blurt, "I didn't know it was a costume party!" But they just stood there, frozen by the blinding glare from the 36C cups pointed at them.

"What's the matter with all of you?" she asked, parading before them like a general inspecting her troops. "If you don't think I should wear the dress to the party, just say so."

Kim MacCauley swallowed hard. "Personally, Ms. Mann, I think it was very thoughtful of you to find a dress that will make our guests feel at home."

Sarina looked down at the dress. Unless home was a bordello, she couldn't imagine it making their Chinese partners feel anything but sorry they'd entered into a joint venture with Global Century. She cocked a skeptical eye at her assistant. "What exactly do you mean, Kim?"

Kim looked around at her colleagues, pleading for help, but they skillfully avoided meeting her eyes. "Well, it's so colorful and...unusual, like those dragons that run through the streets of Chinatown on Chinese New Year."

Hearing a snigger but unable to identify its source, Sarina reluctantly dismissed the women. Obviously, she'd been wrong to assume that just because she welcomed their honest opinions, they felt comfortable giving them. But she wasn't ready to accept Dr. Barrett Brown's view that she couldn't rely on them for companionship.

"Liz?" she called, as the woman who was nearest to her in age and background reached the door. "May I see you for a moment? And close the door, please."

Liz did as she was asked. "If it's about those reports being ready before the Hong Kong group gets in, Ms. Mann—"

"No," Sarina said, as she stuffed the dragon dress back inside its bag. Taking a breath, she turned to the other woman. "I just wondered if you were doing anything tonight."

"I don't think so. Do you need me to stay late?"

"Actually," Sarina began, walking behind her desk and thinking of how to phrase her request. After all, she'd never before asked a staff member to socialize after work. Of course, it wasn't the same as one of them asking her out, but the result would be the same. "There's a movie I've been wanting to see and I thought you might like to join me. We can have dinner first."

Liz Elliot's eyes registered first shock, then discomfort. "That sounds lovely, Ms. Mann, but—"

"You did say you had no plans for the evening, didn't you?"

"Well, I..." Liz held her breath. Then, letting it go, she accepted Sarina's invitation.

Dismissing a squeamishness over having trapped Liz into accepting, Sarina beamed triumphantly. After Liz left her office, she set to poring over the financials on a luxury hotel in Rome she was thinking of acquiring with a relish for her work she hadn't felt in months.

By late afternoon, she'd been so effortlessly productive she was shocked when Kim peeked in to ask if Sarina had any further work for her before she left for the day. Saying she hadn't, and wishing Kim a pleasant evening, Sarina gathered her own coat and bag. Noticing a new lightness in her step, she headed for the door.

So, Dr. Barrett Brown was right. You have been lonely.

Hearing the insufferable voice of her inner know-it-all, Sarina paused. "You again?"

Who else would point out to you that if you hadn't been looking forward to Liz's company tonight, you would have dragged through the afternoon the way you always do.

"And from that you conclude I've been lonely?" Spying a stray file on her desk, Sarina took it to a bank of drawers. "Okay, so maybe Julia had a point when she said I needed to make new friends. I have to admit I'm feeling more energetic than I have in a long time. And I didn't have to call Buddies-By-the-Hour, either."

Friends in High Places. But hey, the important thing is, you might actually sleep tonight.

"Wouldn't that be wonderful?" Sarina stretched as though she already had.

You might even dream you're in the arms of some big, strong—

"Forget it!" Sarina yanked open a file drawer. "I'll be quite content with eight hours of total unconsciousness, thank you. Every night for the rest of my life, as a matter of fact."

As Sarina rifled through the file tabs, all she could see were images of Rance, then of Rance and Jillian in each other's arms on *her* wedding night nearly a year ago. Suddenly, her eyes smarted, burning with tears buried hot and deep, like lava. They so stunned her with their sudden intensity, she nearly allowed them to brim over. Clenching a fist, she swallowed hard. "I won't cry. I won't—"

Hearing the phone and knowing Kim had gone, Sarina walked to her desk and answered the call. "Liz! I was just on my way. I was thinking we might eat at—"

A moment later, Sarina's tone had lost its verve. "No, of course I understand. It's not every day a childhood friend you haven't seen in years comes to town," she said, hanging up and suspecting that Liz's old friend was a concoction.

The problem was, *all* of Sarina's friends were concoctions. She could no longer deny that Dr. Barrett Brown had been right. Corporations were pyramids, and geometrically speaking, the higher one climbed the fewer peers one had, and the harder it was to find simple, undemanding companionship.

Of course, there *was* a solution to her problem. Reaching into her coat pocket, she withdrew a wad of paper, uncrumpled it to reveal a phone number. Then, shaking her head, she crumpled it again. She might be down, but she wasn't desperate. Or was she? Walking to the window, she gazed down on East 57th Street. So many dots scurrying in so many different directions, so many people going so many places. She doubted any of them were free for dinner and a movie.

She doubted she'd sleep tonight.

Returning to her desk, she dialed the number and waited for the recording to beep. "Yes, Friends in High Places? My name is Sarina Mann and—" She took a deep breath, then let it go. "I need a Friend."

As HIS CABBY BABBLED on in a predictably unintelligible dialect, Max Evangelist dispensed with his predictable, appropriately spaced grunts. He was too busy hating his brother-in-law. And the only reason he still thought of Tony Dario as his brother-in-law was that he no longer considered him his best friend. When he had boasted he was so confident of winning their bet that he'd let Tony choose his client, Max never dreamed the dirty cheat would choose a woman.

He'd fought Tony's choice on every imaginable ground, and a few that were better left unimagined. In the first place, he'd argued, the agency had never made an opposite-sex match. But as Tony correctly pointed out, it had no express policy against doing so.

"Just think, Max," Tony had said, propping his legs on his desk. "You'll be going boldly where no Friend has gone before."

"Yeah, like into court." Max pointed at the file Tony had handed him earlier. "Did you stop to think that this Ms. Mann might be one of those militant types who thinks she's being sexually harassed every time a man looks at her?"

"Don't look at her."

Max gave Tony a withering stare.

"You could wear really dark glasses."

"And you can go straight to—"

"Max, Max," Tony said, rising from behind his desk and clapping his arm around Max's shoulder. "You're getting upset for no reason."

"No reason? I can give you three right off the top of my head. One," he said, sticking out his thumb to begin the count. "She's a woman, and two, I'm a man."

Tony looked at the forefinger Max had stopped counting with. "What's the third reason?"

Heaving a sigh, Max shoved his hands in his trousers pockets. "That's just it. I'd rather there not be a third reason."

Tony's laugh started small and grew. "Are you saying you think it's automatically the case that because your client is a woman, you can't have a strictly professional relationship with her? Because if you are, you might as well save us both a lot of trouble and concede right now that I've won the bet."

"The hell I will!" Besides, Max thought, he hadn't been saying that a man and a woman couldn't be just friends, though in his experience, the odds were against it. The typical heterosexual male considered the possibility of having sex with every woman of childbearing age he met. It was in the genes, a mandate to propagate the species. It fell to women to propagate it well. Their genes directed them to choose the heartiest of the available chromosomes, the best providers for and protectors of their offspring.

He wasn't making this up. The research proved it. Anyway, he didn't need a geneticist to tell him what he and every other under-ninety male sweating it out in fitness centers were getting fit for—the women who were pumping iron beside them. Tony knew it, too. "Obviously," Max said, "you're the one who doesn't think it's possible for persons of the opposite sex to have a purely platonic relationship or you wouldn't have matched me up with the sex opposite mine."

Grinning, Tony clapped his hand over his heart. "You wound me, old buddy. Would I, the father of your nephew, do anything so mean, so low, so despicable, just to win our bet?"

Max raised Sarina's file between them. "You've interviewed her, right?"

"Right."

"She's attractive, right?"

"A knockout."

Dropping the file on the chair beside him, Max made a fist, tempted to demonstrate Tony's last word. Suddenly, remembering that the client had the right to reject a Friend following a preliminary meeting, he relaxed. Sarina Mann had requested someone who was sincere; someone who enjoyed intelligent conversation without having to dominate or win points. In other words, she wouldn't be expecting the agency to send a man, nor would she likely take a chance on one. Besides, if she was as attractive as Tony said she was, undoubtedly there'd be a man in her life who would find the arrangement completely out of the question.

On the other hand, what if both she and her significant other had one of those open relationships that allowed pretty much anything you'd find in a Woody Allen film?

She might even *prefer* a male Friend. She might cause him extreme pain every time she crossed her legs in a short skirt, and enjoy doing it.

"Damn you, Tony! You set me up."

Tony feigned an innocent expression. "Max, I only did what I always do when I make a placement. I matched you with the client you had the most in common with."

"Except for our genders," Max replied. Knowing he'd trapped himself into this situation and that a bet was a bet, he made a disgusted face. Retrieving Sarina Mann's file, he headed out of the office. Pointing to Tony's name on the door, he said, "Don't start removing mine from my door yet, pal. The lady still has to approve me."

"Of course," Tony replied. "But if I were you, Max, I wouldn't do anything that might make her decide not to, like picking your nose. As you well know, when a client rejects a Friend, we always ask why."

That's what *he* wanted to know, Max thought, getting out of the cab and looking up at the Global Century Building. Why had he been so stupid as to allow Tony to select his client? Because he'd been determined to prove, unequivocally, that there was no more reason for the Friends to become emotionally involved with their clients than with any other business associate. And he still was.

Maybe he was making too much of his client being a woman, he thought as he handed his card to the receptionist in the lobby and waited for clearance from Sarina Mann's office. Just because Tony had said she was beautiful didn't mean *he* would find her appealing. And even if she did turn his head, he argued as he stepped into the elevator and pressed the button for the fiftieth floor, her habits might turn him off. She did say she wanted a Friend who was a good listener. Maybe she was a talker, the kind who went into detail until eyes glazed over. Or maybe the type who forgot the punch lines to jokes, or worse, had no sense of humor at all.

Maybe, he thought after Sarina Mann's assistant seated him in her department's reception area, she's the insecure kind, needing constant attention, thriving on flattery. No, he decided, observing the impressive number of people she had working at her direction. She hadn't risen to this perch in a multinational corporation because she was insecure—which meant she had to be the complete opposite.

A predator, always on the scent of fresh blood. Despite her avowal of caring and sharing—at least in conversation with Tony—she had gobbled her way up the corporate food chain and was now ruthlessly eliminating her competition for the choicest investment opportunities around the world. By the time the receptionist ushered Max into her office, he expected to see a wild-eyed savage gnawing on the carcass of the last international financier foolish enough to challenge her.

Instead, he found a disarmingly feminine creature—neither too short nor too tall, too round nor too slender. As she walked toward him—a fetching Susan Hayward hitch in her stride—offering her hand and a charmingly tilted smile, he saw nothing sharper than the rays of the gold sunburst pinned to her black jacket. Her suit, while certainly proper business attire, was cut to silhouette a figure that was far more hourglass than time clock. Her blouse—tawny satin, and draping softly from a high neck—set off an equally soft and satiny complexion. Striking blue eyes dominated her heart-shaped face, suggesting a nature that was vibrant but far from feral. The only untamed thing about Sarina Mann was her hair—a thick, lush, mass of waves, burnished red-gold like the finest bourbon and just as intoxicating to his senses. Tony had said, as any sighted man would, that Sarina Mann was a knockout. But to Max, she was more. She was a redhead, and she might as well be pointing a .44 in that hand she was extending to him.

A fate, not incidentally, Max would wish on Tony if the

man weren't responsible for his sister and his nephew. At this very moment, the double-dealer was probably estimating how many seconds it would take for Sarina Mann's glorious hair—not to mention just about everything else Max had seen so far—to win the bet—and the agency—for him.

Unless his appendix burst within the next five seconds, Max calculated, Tony wouldn't have to wait long.

SARINA HAD BEEN surprised when Kim MacCauley announced that a Mr. Evangelist from Friends in High Places was down in reception, asking to see her. She'd met with Tony Dario, the agency's placement director, just yesterday, and given him the information he required to match her with one of their "Friends," as he called them. Sarina laughed to herself, recalling how he'd made the Friends sound like yuppie Quakers, sophisticated yet trustworthy.

Silly, of course. The whole notion of going through an agency to find a trusted companion was a bit silly. Still, trust *was* the issue. Or rather, the lack of it, as Dr. Barrett Brown had pointed out. And as Tony Dario had reasoned, people used agencies to take the guesswork out of finding everything from cooks to nannies to marriage partners, so why not friends? He had assured her that the background of all Friends was checked, and that one would be assigned to her only after a painstaking evaluation of a number of compatibility factors. How many of us, he had asked, could trust that the random people we meet and befriend haven't just gotten out of Leavenworth? How can we be sure that when they ask us to a concert, they aren't talking about a grunge band?

He'd made sense and was himself so likable, she found herself wanting to say, "Great! Send me two." But he'd hardly had time to find one Friend for her, which was perhaps why this Max Evangelist was here. Perhaps he'd been sent to obtain additional information, or to submit her to psychological testing—though she couldn't imagine Dario forgetting to mention the need for it. Nevertheless, the man was here and she might as well see him.

As Liz showed him into her office, Sarina's first thought was that he didn't look like her idea of a psychologist— thin, pale, with an otherworldly look in his eyes. The look in this man's eyes was so definitely of this world, so magnetic, she barely felt her legs beneath her as she moved toward him. The closer she got, the more aware she was that he couldn't possibly spend his entire waking life probing the hidden recesses of the human psyche. His body was too fit, too ramrod straight, its power his to command. Maybe he was really a private investigator sent to ferret out secrets the agency would want to know before processing her application, like whether or not she kept a bullwhip in her desk. But she doubted P.I.s wore hand-tailored suits.

No, this man was accustomed to buttery-soft leather shoes, not gumshoes. He had a discerning eye, all right, but for the best of everything, not the kinds of things normally found in a gutter. His eyes, in fact, were like cognac, warm and penetrating, and intriguingly darker than his golden-brown hair. It was thick, that hair, and brushed back from a cerebral forehead that effectively eliminated all possibility that he was only an empty, gray, pin-striped Italian suit.

Sarina couldn't imagine what he wanted with her. Actually, as she clasped his hand and felt the surge of his high-rpm drive, she began to imagine a scintillating array of things she wished he wanted with her, none of them having to do with either psychology or friendship. She hadn't reacted with this intensity to any man since Rance, and perhaps not even to him. So the sooner she discovered his reason for being here and got rid of him, the better. Spending five minutes with Max Evangelist would undoubtedly stir up more trouble than attending next week's gala in her Chinese-dragon dress.

Sarina withdrew her hand with some reluctance. Noting that, she remained close to the door, as much to be near an exit as to encourage him to state his business quickly and leave. "Is there some problem with my application for a Friend, Mr. Evangelist?"

Yes, Max thought. When you checked the box indicating your sex, you should have crossed out "female" and written in "All Woman."

"No, no problem," he said, unable to think of what to say next, other than, "Will you marry me?" But Sarina Mann wouldn't even consider a man who'd been stupid enough to lose his entire business on a bet, and that was exactly what he was going to do if he didn't pull himself together. "Ms. Mann," he said, gazing into incredibly and hypnotically blue eyes. "I'm your Friend."

And I'm your slave, Sarina thought, bathing him in a mesmerized gaze. Suddenly, she realized what he'd meant. "Oh, you mean you're my *Friend.*" Her eyes popped. "*You're* my Friend?"

"That's right," Max replied, feeling as if he was doing the sequel to *Mission Impossible—Mission Utterly Impossible.* "I've been assigned to you."

Sarina's mouth fell open. She could think of a number of assignments for him, but going with her to see the Knicks wasn't one of them. "There must be some mistake," she said, retreating behind the battlement of her desk. "From what Mr. Dario said yesterday, I gathered it would take some time to make an appropriate match."

"Mr. Dario..." Max began, walking toward her, treading on images of his former best friend's face, "was correct. It just so happened that I not only shared your areas of expertise and interests, but was immediately available." *For destruction.*

Slowly, Sarina sank into her chair, wondering what she

was going to tell Tony Dario when she rejected Max Evangelist. "He's a man—I mean, you're a man," she said, looking up and meeting his espresso gaze, drinking in the heat.

And he's a gorgeous man, too, Sarina.

Hearing her libidinous alter ego, Sarina made fists. *Not now,* she commanded it.

If not now, when? You're not getting any younger, you know.

If I'm not getting younger, she shot back, *neither are you.*

My point exactly. I'm tired of waiting for you to get over your fear of romance. I'm dying in here!

Be patient, she ordered her nagging subconscious. *I'm about to finish the job.*

Beginning, she decided, with eliminating as much of Max Evangelist's physical advantage over her as possible. She shot to her feet.

But Max, who found he wanted to peer directly into her eyes, aquatic blue and sparkling like the gemlike waters off Grand Cayman, was at the same time taking the seat behind him. When he looked across her desk and met not her eyes but her feminine curves, he also met with a difficult choice. What would it be, mesmerizing eyes or luscious curves? Finally, he did the gentlemanly thing and rose.

But Sarina, reacting to his having taken a seat, sat down again. When she gazed across her desk, she found herself staring at abs that were as on the level as the pope. Quickly shifting her gaze upward, she broadened it to take in his chest and shoulders, and deepened it with admiration for the lay of his powder-blue, subtly checked shirt, the deftly made knot in his gold-and-charcoal silk tie, and the confident style in the powder-blue kerchief in his breast pocket. There was no denying he was an imposing figure of a man, and as delightful as it would undoubtedly be, she'd be damned if she'd allow him to impose that figure on her.

"Have a seat, Mr. Evangelist," she said, "before one of us slips a disc."

So much for hoping that Sarina Mann had no sense of humor, Max thought, blinded by the twinkle in her eye. But he was still hopeful he'd never have to succumb to the delights of sharing laughter with her. When she'd pointed out that he was a man, she had to be imagining what the man in her life would have to say about Max being her Friend. He knew that if he were lucky enough to be that man, the only other male he'd allow her to befriend would be a ninety-year-old monk. Make that ninety-five. And light in the sandals.

"I can certainly understand your finding an opposite-sex arrangement unacceptable," he said, anxious to wrap up this meeting and escape to safer ground.

"No, it's not that," Sarina replied. She didn't want to appear to be one of those primitivists who thought sex was always lurking in the shadows of every relationship between men and women. Besides, she'd certainly had her share of male buddies, especially in college. Of course, none of them had looked remotely like Max Evangelist, but technically, they provided evidence that purely platonic relationships between men and women were possible. Drawing a cigarette from the case atop her desk, she placed it between her fingers.

Instinctively, Max reached into his pocket for his lighter and leaning toward Sarina, flicked it.

"No thanks," Sarina said, waving him off. "I don't smoke."

Max's brows lifted, but he asked no questions. If Sarina Mann insisted on being sexy, smart, funny, *and* fascinating in a quirky sort of way, he had no choice but to get the heck away from her. Fast. But how? Suddenly, the answer came from something the damnable woman herself had said. "I'm terribly sorry, Ms. Mann. I can't understand how Mr. Dario could have matched a nonsmoker with a cigar smoker. So, I'll just be on my way and ask Mr. Dario to find you a—"

"Please don't blame Mr. Dario," Sarina said. "I did tell him I wouldn't automatically reject a smoker." *If I'd known he was going to send you, I'd have told him I shoot smokers on sight.* She put the cigarette down. "I'm curious, Mr. Evangelist. Is it usual for the agency to arrange friendships between men and women?"

"I wouldn't say it's usual. More like something we're betting will work."

Sarina swiveled to one side. If the agency was gambling on opposite-sex friendships succeeding, it had certainly stacked the odds against itself by sending Max Evangelist into the field. She couldn't imagine forgetting for a single moment that he was a devastatingly attractive man, which meant she could no more let down her guard with him than she could with a reporter from the *Wall Street Journal.* The last thing she'd want him to know was that she was not only a high-powered, globe-trotting executive, but also a loveless, friendless insomniac plagued by a curse. Although she wished the agency and Max all the luck in the world, they were going to have to put their money on another filly. Unless—

"Are you married, Mr. Evangelist?"

Max hesitated. Her question was unexpected, but logical, under the circumstances. "No."

Damn. Sarina was well aware of the pain that comes with discovering your husband has cheated on you—even if he's only been your husband for six hours—and she also knew she could never do unto another woman as Jillian had done unto her. Married men were the least of her temptations. But Max Evangelist had the audacity to look and sound and move like temptation incarnate *and* not be married. All, however, was not lost. Mentally crossing her fingers, she asked, "In a relationship, then?"

To be truthful, Max knew he ought to say that for the

last six weeks, he'd been so busy expanding the agency
that he hadn't even had a date. As much as he hated playing
fast and loose with the truth, he was more worried about
the shambles Tony would make of the agency after Max
had lost the bet. Besides, he was in relationships with a lot
of people. His sister for one, or rather—in Mike's case—
two.

"You could say that," he replied.

The relief Sarina had hoped for failed to materialize.
"You could say that" and "forsaking all others" were not
quite the same thing. Even if she could pretend they were,
would his lover take so benign a view of their Friendship?
Would she do nothing while some other woman bared her
soul to him?

More likely his lover would be the jealous type, and her
bare *body* would end up with a hole in it.

Suddenly she realized he'd said something. "I'm sorry,
Mr. Evangelist. Would you mind repeating that?"

Actually, I would, Max thought. Asking the first time and
priming himself for a disheartening answer hadn't been
easy. "I said, are you?"

"Am I what?"

Poor darling, Max thought. She was showing all the
signs of executive stress—the inability to concentrate, and
that bit with the cigarette was probably no quirk but
strained nerves. He knew exactly what she was going
through and suddenly, he wanted to take care of her. Looking at her now, he had the strangest feeling that she be-
longed to him. Unable to accept that she might be married
or engaged, or even in a relationship, he said, "Seeing anyone."

Sarina's pride couldn't bear for him to know the truth,
that she'd been jilted, and on her wedding night. End of
story. "You could say that," she replied. She was seeing
Dr. Barrett Brown, wasn't she?

Max knew he should have expected as much. Still, all

he could manage to utter was an "Oh," which sounded the way it felt. Final.

A strained silence hung between them. Sarina supposed nothing remained for her to say, except thanks but no thanks, and goodbye. So, why was she finding it so hard? One thing was certain, delaying the inevitable wouldn't make things any easier. Picking up the cigarette and turning it end over end, she said, "Mr. Evangelist, I've enjoyed meeting you, but I'm afraid—" The phone rang.

Sarina excused herself to answer. After taking the call from Liz, she looked at Max apologetically. "I'm sorry. We're working a deal in Rome and some data's come through I need to take a look at." Pushing away from her desk, she rose.

Max also stood, frustrated by the interruption of his dismissal. "But—"

"I'll just be a moment," she said, making for the door.

Watching her adorable walk, Max realized that as desperate as he was for her to be done with him, he didn't want to leave without looking at her—really looking at her—one last time. Without forever etching her beguiling loveliness into his memory. Just once more, he wanted to hear her sultry voice, sample her wit—and inhale her scent, which instantaneously transported him from Manhattan to the exquisite jasmine gardens he'd once visited in the Orient.

Perhaps he might even hear her laughter. He was sure it had to be deep—a woman like her could never be a giggler—and infectious. And strangely, he wanted to find out what made her cry, even though few things disconcerted him more than a female with mascara running down her cheeks. Beyond that, he didn't even want to think about all that he would never know about Sarina Mann.

"I'll be waiting," he said, holding her gaze with his as she paused halfway to the door.

"I'm glad," Sarina replied softly.

Tearing his gaze from the sight of her, Max glanced at his watch and recalled that he had promised his sister he would come for dinner that evening. Given his current low regard for her husband, Max thought it best that he and Tony keep their distance for a while. He couldn't risk Mike's getting caught in the cross fire that was bound to erupt between her brother and her blockhead of a husband. He hated to disappoint her by canceling out for the third time in a month, but it was better than chancing her going into premature labor. Stopping Sarina at the door, he asked to use the phone.

"Just hit nine for an outside line," she said, and stepping into the hall, left the door slightly ajar behind her.

After Sarina left, Max dialed Mike's number, then waited while she took her time getting rid of a call on the other line. When she returned, the excuse he gave her for begging off dinner was the one he'd truthfully given her twice before, that he had a lot of paperwork to catch up on. She wasn't buying it now, either.

"What do you mean, I don't want to spend time with you?" he asked. Lord, she was sensitive. Of course, she was sensitive, he chided himself. Wouldn't he be a little cranky if he'd been living *Invasion of the Body Snatchers* for seven months? "That's ridiculous, Mike. But...Mike... How can you even say a thing like that?"

Sarina returned from Liz Elliot's office. As she reached for the knob on her door, she summoned the courage to march in and turn Max Evangelist's Friendship down. But, picking up his half of what sounded like a distressing phone conversation, she let go of the handle. If he didn't resolve his differences with whoever this guy Mike was in another second or two, she'd do the polite thing and wait out of earshot.

"Mike... But... Of course I still love you! I've never stopped loving you and I never will."

Her eyes popping, Sarina forgot her contempt for eavesdroppers and pressed her ear to the crack between the door and the jamb.

"I told you the reason I can't have dinner with you is that I have to work late," Max said. "No! It's not because I can't stand seeing you fat. Mike... Mike... You're not fat, okay!"

Men didn't get apoplectic about a few extra pounds, Sarina thought. Mike must be a nickname for the woman Max was seeing. And from the sound of things, not for much longer. Squinting through the opening, barely breathing, she watched Max brush back his hair in obvious exasperation. Then she saw him smile—tenderly, she thought. "You just have a little potbelly," he said into the receiver.

Blinking, Sarina straightened. If Mike was a woman, Max would have been talking thighs, not bellies. Which could mean just one thing. Mike was a man and Max Evangelist was—

Gape-mouthed, Sarina took another hard look at Max—at the commanding breadth of his shoulders; the boldness of his gestures; the confidence in his bearing. His features were chiseled, and might have been sharp if not for that incredible smile—dazzling, warm, rakish. *Sexy.* To her. She took her pulse. As she expected, it was somewhere between elevated and we're gonna have a hot time in the old town tonight. *He* can't *be gay.*

"Yes, Mike, I hear you. I know you went to a lot of trouble," Max said, rolling his eyes. "My favorite dish...wine...flowers...candles."

I guess he can, Sarina decided. Dumbstruck, she backed away from the door.

She'd known other gay men, some of them as handsome as Max if not more so. But she'd always felt asexual around them, as if her own heterosexuality had been neutralized. And this distinct lack of sexual attraction was, in its own way, pleasant. It was amazing how much fun men and women could have together when sex wasn't an issue.

But from the moment she had first seen Max Evangelist, sex was very much an issue, at least for her. How could she have been so mistaken about him, about the electricity she'd felt when he'd taken her hand in his, the kind of charge that only happens when opposites attract? *Maybe that's what happens after nearly a year of enforced celibacy,* she thought. Making a note to discuss her unreliable sensors with Dr. Barrett Brown, she collected herself sufficiently to proceed with dismissing Max as her Friend.

But as she raised her hand to push open the door, she stopped. What was wrong with her? Hadn't her sole objection to Max being her companion just been eliminated? If they had as much in common as he claimed, why not give him a chance? He was obviously an intelligent man, cultured, gentlemanly. Fit. He might make a wonderful playmate on the slopes or jogging in the park. Of course, there was one sure way to find out whether or not Max Evangelist was the right Friend for her.

Reentering her office, she smiled as she approached Max, delightedly noting that he didn't fail to rise upon seeing her. She knew very few straight men who would have done the same. "Mr. Evangelist, before I let you go," she said, walking to her credenza and removing a shopping bag, "there's something I need to know."

Max swallowed, amazed at how much it hurt to realize that after today, he'd never see Sarina Mann again. "Shoot," he said. *Preferably, at my heart. Put it out of its misery.*

Sarina pulled a neon-colored garment out of the bag in her hand.

"My God!" Max came close to shrieking as he gazed at the hideous dress. "Tell me you're not actually planning to wear that…thing."

"Does that mean you don't like it?"

"Like it?" He didn't suppose insulting her at this point was really cheating on his bet, since she'd already decided to reject him. Lowering his head, he covered his eyes. "I've seen drain clogs I liked better."

Dropping the dress in the bag, Sarina stared at Max with total admiration. He was a truly honest man and would make a trustworthy Friend. Of course, technically, he could pull a Jillian on her, she supposed. But then, he had Mike, and she was off romance for good, anyway. So what could be better than a best friend who won't ask to borrow your most expensive little black dress? "Mr. Evangelist...Max," she began, turning and starting toward him.

As she neared, Max seemed to stiffen. "Ms. Mann, I believe you were about to tell me you'd come to the conclusion that I'm not exactly the kind of Friend you're looking for."

Sarina couldn't help but notice that her nearness appeared to make him jittery. She wondered if he'd had a domineering mother. No, too *Psycho*. He was probably just uncomfortable around women whom he hadn't yet outed himself to. Hoping to calm him, she laid her hand on his forearm. "On the contrary, Max. I think you'll make a perfect companion. Please tell Mr. Dario I approve."

Max felt his heart thud. What had happened in the last five minutes to make her change her mind? Didn't she care that he'd just compared her dress—unfavorably—to a scummy hairball? Didn't she care that he was a *he*? "But...but what about the fact that I'm a—"

"Oh, that's no problem," Sarina said.

"It isn't?" Max hated to admit it, but his ego felt the sting of her nonchalance. If it wasn't a problem for her that he was a man, he was either losing his grip, or worse, his hair. Certainly, nothing had alleviated the problem she posed for him. And the way she was talking, his problems were only going to get worse. "But—"

"Max, don't apologize," Sarina said, perching on the corner of her desk and fixing him with an earnest gaze. "I admit I assumed the agency would send a woman, but you can tell Mr. Dario that I think his sending you was a stroke of sheer genius.''

Stroke is definitely the operative word, Max thought, feeling his temples throb and his skin flush, whether from the mention of Tony's name or the sight of Sarina Mann's shapely legs, he wasn't sure. "Ms. Mann—"

"You might as well start calling me Sarina."

Max released the breath he'd been holding. "Sarina, are you sure you don't want to take a few days to think about this?"

"Oh, I'm quite sure," she replied, walking behind her desk. "Once I make up my mind about something, I don't change it."

Somehow, he'd known that about her. Unable to see any way of extricating himself from what was quickly turning out to be his worst nightmare, Max resigned himself to the inevitable. "That's it, then," he said, envisioning the agency sprouting wings and flying away. Leaning over Sarina's desk, he offered her his hand.

"I guess you could say I've just become Mann's Best Friend.''

3

THAT NIGHT, Sarina slept. And every night for the next four, when she turned out the light on the Hepplewhite chest beside her bed, she fell instantly into a deep, delicious, uninterrupted sleep.

I feel like a new woman, she thought as she padded to the kitchen after a fifth blissful night in the arms of the god of sleep. A woman who'd been blessed with a miracle, though she suspected the real reason for her sudden restfulness had more to do with an Evangelist named Max rather than Matthew, Mark, Luke, or John.

Although an endless string of meetings with visiting associates had kept her from availing herself of Max's services, for the past five days she'd no longer felt quite so alone in the world, so friendless. Max was there for her, his companionship on call. The best part was that with Max Evangelist, professional friend, she didn't have to watch her back. And she certainly didn't have to watch her heart. All she had to keep an eye on was how much she was spending for his Friendship.

On the other hand, she thought as she set her coffee grinder whirring and inhaled deeply of the scent of French roast, could she really put a price on sleep and the increased productivity that followed a full eight hours of it? What *wouldn't* she pay to enjoy lunch conversation that didn't sound as though it had been scripted by the Financial News Network? In contrast to that alternative, the lunch date she had made with Max yesterday for 1:00 P.M. today would be a bargain, even at the Four Seasons' prices.

All in all, Sarina decided as she sliced a bagel, things were looking up for the first time since her disastrous wedding night nearly a year ago. At her next therapy session, she'd have to thank Dr. Barrett Brown for recommending Friends in High Places. "Doctor, you won't believe this," she'd say, "but since the day I met my Friend, I haven't lost a minute's sleep. I'm cured of insomnia."

But if that was true, Sarina thought as she took the light cream cheese from the refrigerator, she really didn't need another therapy session. All she had to do was phone her gratitude to Julia Barrett Brown. And with the money she'd have spent in therapy, discussing her nonexistent hostilities, she'd splurge on a new outfit for her upcoming trip to Rome. Heck, a whole new wardrobe. Better yet, she'd take Max along to shop for it.

Twenty minutes later, fed, dressed, and amazingly light-hearted, Sarina prepared to leave for the office. Checking her purse and seeing that her silver cigarette case was empty, she dashed to the antique secretary where she kept a carton. Turning the brass key to lower the top, she paused. If she could sleep through the night, she could certainly get through the day without having to tote around cigarettes she never smoked.

Locking the secretary, she headed for the door.

So, what do you think the dream meant?

Hearing her inner analyst, Sarina came to a stop. "What dream? And you'd better make this quick. I have a staff meeting in forty minutes."

The dream you had last night, Sarina. About you and Max. And don't tell me you don't remember it.

Sarina's stomach lurched with incipient panic. Nevertheless, she saw no real reason to adjust her level of optimism, yet. "Of course I don't remember it. That's because it never happened. Don't you think that if I had dreamed about Max Evangelist and me I'd have remembered it?''

Look, Sarina, I'm your subconscious mind and if you tell me pigs fly, I'm supposed to believe you. But I have to tell you, kid, nobody does denial like you do.

Shoulders slumping, her purse slipping to the floor, Sarina plopped in the chair beside the door. ''What *did* I dream last night?''

Well, you and Max were in a meadow, cavorting like a couple of leftover flower children.

Sarina sneered. Already this dream had all the signs of having resulted more from the Szechuan pork she'd eaten for dinner than from repressed urges. Cavorting, much less in love beads, wasn't her style. ''Go on.''

Suddenly, the two of you came to a stream. You crossed it alone. Then you dipped your cupped hands into the water and drank.

Sarina shrugged. ''I imagine all that cavorting made me thirsty.'' Looking at her watch, she hoisted her purse onto her shoulder and rose. ''Now, if you don't mind, I have a bus to—''

Do you know what you did then?

Sarina propped her hand on her waist. ''The Bugaloo?''

You called to Max to cross the stream and take a drink from your hands.

''Well, he'd been cavorting, too, hadn't he?'' Sarina rolled her eyes.

Don't you get it?

''Frankly, no I don't.'' Sarina unlocked her door.

Water is a symbol of many things—among them, eroticism. You crossed the sexual waters, Sarina, and sampled them—as we both know you've done—

''I've never heard you complain.''

And you beckoned to Max to come taste the waters, too. Now I ask you, doesn't that give you pause?

Sarina did pause, but not for long. ''You wouldn't by

any chance be trying to tell me that I haven't really accepted that Max Evangelist is gay?''

No, dear. I'm telling you that I haven't accepted it. I have an instinct about these things. Remember Jack, next door? Didn't I clue you in that he was gay even before he asked you where you stood in the waxing-versus-shaving debate?

"True," Sarina said, locking up her apartment and striding toward the atrium. "But Max asked me if I minded that he was gay, don't you remember?"

As I recall, you interrupted him. He may have been about to ask if you minded that he was a man.

"You heard his phone conversation with Mike as clearly as I did," Sarina said, pulling on her gloves while she waited for the elevator. "How could you possibly have any doubt that he's romantically involved with another man?"

"I *don't* have any doubt."

Unless her subconscious was coming down with a cold, the last voice Sarina heard was definitely male. She glanced to her right. "Oh, good morning, Jack," she said as the elevator opened. She stepped inside, and Jack joined her.

"You're talking about the new tenant on the first floor, of course," he said, pressing the button for the lobby. "And you're right. He's as gay as a lark. I ought to know, though sadly," he added with a sigh, "my knowledge isn't of a personal nature." When the elevator opened at the lobby, he told Sarina to have a fab day and exited, leaving her utterly speechless.

And motionless until the doors began to whoosh shut. Forcing them apart, she left the building. Immediately, she turned her collar up against a swirl of flurries as she set out toward the bus stop, pondering Jack's revelation about the new tenant. Apparently, she was surrounded by attractive men and in absolutely no danger of finding romance with any of them. Comforted, she smiled despite the cold.

But what if her subconscious had been right? she thought

as she boarded the Lexington Avenue bus and dropped her token into the slot. What if she'd somehow misconstrued Max's conversation with "Mike," who could be every inch a woman, albeit one whose weight collected in her mid-section. From what Sarina had overheard, Max's relationship with this cherub-shaped woman had been less than heavenly. Which meant that Max might soon be free. Heck, he could be free right now.

"Damn," Sarina said, as she stepped off the bus. A straight Max Evangelist was neither gay nor funny. In fact, he was outright dangerous. Entering the Global Century Building, she wondered what excuse she would give him for breaking their lunch date. For ending their Friendship before it had even begun. Shoving open the glass door to her department, she stalked past her assistant, unlocked her office and slammed the door behind her. Dumping the contents of her purse on her desk, she grabbed her cigarette case. Finding it empty because, as she only now recalled, she'd adventurously left home without refilling it, she flung it atop the heap of purse junk. "Damn," she repeated, then reached for the phone to call Friends in High Places.

MAX ENTERED the Four Seasons at precisely 1:00 P.M. At fifteen seconds after one, he did an about-face and retreated outside to East 52nd Street.

Not that he wasn't hungry. He was, in fact, famished. He hadn't eaten since yesterday morning, when Sarina Mann had called to arrange this Friendly little lunch, shattering his delusion that she'd somehow forgotten they'd ever met. How *could* he have eaten when the very pillars of his existence were under assault? Not only was his relationship with Mike and his lifelong friendship with her husband on shaky ground, but now he stood to lose the business he had founded. His only hope was to prove that he could be a Friend and *only* a Friend to five feet, three inches of redheaded temptation.

So, why didn't he just save himself a lot of time and heartache, concede defeat and the business to Tony, put his very pregnant sister at ease about his love for her, and get as far away from Sarina Mann as possible? After all, he was thinking of *her* welfare, too. He ought to step aside and let Tony find her a true Friend, one who wouldn't be imagining how she'd feel in his arms the whole time she was describing the details of her latest merger. Besides, he'd already decided to do as much this morning, after what had been, without question, the worst night's sleep he'd had in nearly a week of restless nights.

Come to think of it, last night he hadn't slept at all. Every time he'd closed his eyes, he'd seen Sarina, luminous, laughing, her hair a halo of fire beneath the sun. He'd pictured her in a meadow, of all places. She'd been dressed in jeans and an oversized shirt—one of his shirts!—looking adorable and running in slow motion through a sea of wild-flowers. And what had he been doing? Running after her, what else?

But that hadn't been the worst of his fantasy. He'd actually caught her, lifting her by the waist as easily as plucking a petal from one of the wild blooms. He'd twirled her around and around, freeing a contagion of laughter from deep inside her, and when she'd pleaded with him to stop, he'd made her promise not to run from him again. She'd promised, but when he'd set her down, she hadn't taken off as he'd expected. She'd turned to him, her gaze entranc-ing, her lips plump and dewy. Pressing against him, she'd reached up and raked her fingers through his hair, along the side of his head to the nape of his neck. Just thinking about it now stirred his blood. Remembering how she'd then cupped the back of his head and lowered it toward hers as she offered up her succulent mouth, he responded as he had in his midnight mirage. He inhaled the spell cast by her magical scent and closing his eyes, surrendered to her irresistible sorcery.

Badly jostled, Max looked around him. But merely returning his sight to the gray reality of winter in New York, letting in the blare of traffic, wasn't enough to break the grip of his daydream. Returning to that improbable meadow, this time as an observer, he could see Sarina bringing her lips to his. His eyes were closed and he raised his arms to encircle her, to crush her to him, his own lips parting in anticipation of a feast. Then she shoved on his chest with all her strength and, laughing like a vixen, ran away. He was stunned, but only for a second. Regaining his balance, he chased her, and this time he tackled her, bringing her down on top of him as he fell to the ground. Over and over they rolled, clinging to each other, legs entwining. Like a couple of adolescents in some stupid coming-of-age flick!

Max brushed back his hair, at last coming to grips with the real world in the form of cold, wet specks of snow. He was a hardened, cynical, native New Yorker, for Pete's sake. What had he been doing traipsing the streets of midtown Manhattan for the last three hours—chilled, hungry and sleep-deprived—trying to shake a ridiculous erotic fantasy?

A Friendship with Sarina Mann was completely out of the question, Max decided once and for all. Stepping to the curb, he scanned the traffic for a taxi to take him back to the office, where he would do the only deed that could save him from a redheaded sorceress and the damage she was inflicting on his savvy self-image. He would surrender Friends in High Places to Tony.

WENDING HER WAY toward the Four Seasons through the coursing midday throng, Sarina had no difficulty instantly singling Max out from an army of camel-coated movers and shakers. His unconventional handsomeness was arresting, the kind that made a woman look twice because once wasn't enough to appreciate the subtle intricacies of his

features or the understated but distinctive touches that were
his style. Like the cashmere scarf draped around his neck,
a brilliant royal blue with random squares in earthy sienna
tones. No woman could catch sight of Max Evangelist and
not feel compelled to know him. Still, it wasn't only his
fascinating looks that had immediately identified him to
Sarina. It was the way her pulse had spiked the moment
she laid eyes on him.

Halting, she turned away. Did she really require proof
beyond her thumping heartbeat to convince her that as long
as there was a chance that Max Evangelist was straight, a
friendship with him was completely out of the question?
Having savored the unsurpassable joy of getting more than
forty winks a night, she wasn't about to give up a single
wink over a libido in limbo. Nor was she about to endure
any more dreams like the one she'd had last night. As suit-
able a companion as Max might be, she'd have to tell him
she'd changed her mind about employing him. She'd have
told him sooner if she could have reached him at his office
this morning. She'd have avoided the stress of seeing him
again. For the last time.

Turning, she gazed at him, her heart going suddenly and
strangely soft, as though the thought of never seeing him
again saddened her. As though, inexplicably, she'd already
begun to care about him as a person instead of viewing him
only as a hazard to the heart. With even more incredulity,
she realized tears had formed in her eyes. Horrified, she
blinked them away. She'd thought she needed no further
evidence that Max Evangelist posed a threat to the maxi-
mum-security confines of her heart, but there it was in her
unbidden tears. The man had to go. Marching up to him,
she tapped him on the shoulder.

"Hello, Max," she said in a very businesslike tone. "I
hope I haven't kept you waiting long."

Hearing Sarina's voice, the throaty tones that issued so
incongruously and so erotically from that slender throat,

feeling her touch, which sent a thrill even through layers of clothing, Max stiffened his spine in order to face her. But his mettle melted like ice in August the moment his gaze landed on those big, blue eyes of hers, all that was visible above the coat collar she held gathered against the cold.

Oddly, *he* was no longer cold at all. Looking at Sarina, he felt the warmth of a sun that only seconds ago hadn't been shining. The arctic gale that had been performing a skin peel on him now wafted across his cheek like the kiss of a gentle breeze. And the bits of white cresting the red-amber waves atop Sarina's head weren't ice crystals but petals from the daisies he was lying amidst with her.

"No, I haven't been waiting long at all, Sarina," Max said, "though I wouldn't mind waiting any amount of time for you." He couldn't believe he'd actually said something so stupid and adolescent. Nor could he believe how blissfully lovestruck he felt. "Hungry?"

Sarina's resolve to dismiss Max before lunch evaporated as she felt his gaze snuggle around her like a down comforter, full of warmth and protection from the harsh realities of a cold and competitive world, a world where glances were weapons and anyone might be the enemy. She still found him much too attractive for comfort, but one thing was certain, Max wasn't an enemy type. As for the tears in her eyes a moment ago, they had undoubtedly come in response to a blast of wind in her face. So, what harm could there possibly be in having one little lunch with him before they parted company? She owed him that much for his trouble, for waiting for her in the snow. Besides, walking over here, she'd worked up quite an appetite.

Sarina released her collar, revealing a mouth Max couldn't help thinking was as much made to be devoured as to devour. She smiled and said, "I could eat a horse."

Holding the door open as she passed before him, he cast doleful eyes heavenward. *And I could end up eating crow.*

AFTER GIVING HER ORDER to the waiter, Sarina focused on Max. Crossing her arms, she arched one brow. "So, Mr. Evangelist, with a name like that, just how high up are your friends?"

Pressing his mated forefingers to lips that hinted of amusement, Max returned Sarina's gaze. "Oh, you'd be surprised at the lofty company I keep. My office is on the thirty-second floor."

Sarina smiled as she buttered a hot, crusty roll, then pinned Max with an even more probing look. "I was referring to your clients. Are they all captains of industry? No politicians or superstars who are adored by millions and loved by no one in particular?"

Max cocked his head to one side. "Do I detect a hint of sarcasm in those velvet tones, Ms. Mann?"

Sarina's breath caught. *Velvet tones?* A decidedly flirtatious choice of words. Not a come-on, perhaps, but an indication that he'd found her voice attractive. Perhaps.

Seeing a cloud of perplexity at his last remark scud across Sarina's face, Max glanced away. Somehow, he had to stop thinking of her as a woman. Or was he supposed to stop thinking of himself as a man? But then again, why should he? he asked with a lift of his brows. As soon as this lunch was over, wasn't he going to find Tony and turn over his keys to the office? Of course, if he did that, then he'd be free to pursue Sarina and—

What? Ask her out? She could turn him down flat. He hadn't considered that. He could wave the white flag at Tony only to discover that Sarina Mann wasn't the least bit attracted to him. All that cavorting with her in the fields of his libidinous imagination had caused him to forget that she'd already told him she was seeing someone. No, he couldn't forfeit his business—his baby—to his brother-in-law's mismanagement over a ridiculously pubescent fantasy. That left him two choices. Whenever he was with Sarina, he had to find a way to either neuter his psyche—

the very words made him shiver—or to neutralize the effect of her charms. Turning his gaze toward her, he tried picturing her with a mustache.

Perhaps misinterpreting his look, Sarina said, "I'm sorry, Max. I shouldn't have poked fun at your clients. After all, I'm one of them." She took a bite from her roll.

Max didn't respond, still a little preoccupied with mentally shading her upper lip with hair. But before he could finish his artwork, he found his gaze wandering to the tip of her nose, probably the most beautifully shaped nose tip he'd ever seen.

Discomfited by Max's stare, Sarina dabbed her napkin over her mouth. She probably had a bread crumb stuck in the corner of it, or maybe a smear of butter was glistening on her chin. But when she'd swiped her face clean, he persisted in looking at her as though she'd sprouted a mustache.

"Of course, I'm not asking you to drop names," she said, fishing in her purse, which lay on the seat beside her, for her compact. "I certainly wouldn't want you mentioning my name to your other clients." Withdrawing the compact, Sarina held it low, flipped it open and snatched a glance at her reflection. It was debris-free, and since they hadn't yet had their salads, she didn't have to check to know there was no lettuce between her teeth. Shutting the compact, she shifted her position. Maybe the light was striking her at an unflattering angle. "I was just wondering how you like your job. You know, being a Friend to so many fascinating people. Not that I'm saying *I'm* fascinating or anything."

Sarina lowered her forehead to her fingertips. She couldn't believe she'd said something so sophomoric. What was the matter with her? At a conference table, she could bend ten men to her will with her conviction and self-assured delivery. But sitting across this one small dining table from this one man, finding herself the object of this one man's scrutiny, she was unraveling. That was simply unacceptable.

"Max," she began, groping for her purse in order to replace her compact. "Is there some reason for your staring at me that I ought to know?"

Yes, Max thought. *You ought to know that when you speak, your eyes flicker and flare like Fourth of July sparklers. Your whole face lights up, and when you punctuate your words with a tilt of your chin or a small shake of your head, I find a new and lovelier facet of that face. Your hair has a life of its own, which you probably know. But what you don't know is that it changes hues as it defies the discipline you've tried to impose on it. Nor can you imagine how much I want to bury my fingers in it.*

But unable to tell her any of what he was thinking, he merely said, "I'm sorry if I made you uncomfortable, Sarina. I was only trying to give you my undivided attention, but I guess I went overboard." Max leaned closer, his voice dropping to a level of confidentiality. "The trouble is, I'm new at this. I've never been a Friend before."

All at once, Sarina's eyes widened and her purse tumbled to the floor. Instinctively, she leaned over to retrieve it, as did Max. Their hands met, then their astonished gazes. They remained momentarily magnetized to one another, then Sarina swallowed and said, "You mean, I'm your first client?"

Max handed Sarina her purse, then they both sat up. Gauging the look on her face, he concluded she wasn't exactly pleased at his revelation. Of course she wasn't pleased. She was hardly the kind of woman who was used to dealing with novices, tolerating their ineptitude, subjecting herself to their learning curve. If only he'd thought to confess at their initial meeting that when it came to Friendship, he was a virgin, she'd have rejected him on the spot. Tony would have assigned him another client, he'd have gotten all the sleep he needed, and while he might have had one small erotic fantasy about Sarina Mann, it wouldn't have turned into a serial. Ah well, better to be rejected late than never.

"You're my very first," he said. Chuckling to himself, he added, "I hope you don't mind."

Mind? Sarina made fists. *I most certainly do mind!* How dare he inform her that she was his very first client just as she was about to fire him? Now she had to consider that if she rejected him on his maiden voyage into Friendship, his superiors would naturally take note. He was probably required to survive a probationary period, and her rejection certainly wasn't going to improve his chances. He might even lose his job, no questions asked.

And for what reason? All because she couldn't keep her pulse from racing off with her better judgment every time she got near him. How selfish could she be?

Taking a breath, she tried to figure some way she could keep Max as her Friend and at the same time, keep her hormones under control. If only she could clear up her confusion about his sexuality. If only she could be sure that the Mike who'd prepared a romantic dinner for him was a man, then she could help her pulse to adjust its throttle.

"I suppose I *was* expecting a more seasoned Friend," she began.

Max began to taste rejection. Freedom. The end of cavorting and the return of blessed sleep. "Does that mean you've changed your mind about me?"

Sarina held her breath, then delivered a definite "Yes."

Max exhaled his relief. He was a reprieved man. Lifting his water glass, he said, "Well, you win some, you lose—"

"I mean, no!"

Max choked in midswallow, water dribbling embarrassingly from the corners of his mouth. "What?"

"I mean—" As the waiter placed a cup of coffee before her, Sarina lifted the creamer. *I mean I'm not sure whether*

I've changed my mind or not. How could she be, when she was of so many different minds about him?

Yet, they all agreed on one thing. Max Evangelist was an honest and sincere human being. He didn't have to tell her that he was a neophyte at Friendship. He could have concocted an international clientele and she would have never known the difference. Instead, he'd told her the truth. He'd admitted there was something he wasn't expert at. Not an easy thing for any man, regardless of his sexual preference, to do.

Still, if his preference ran in her direction, could she disregard that fact? Judging by her instinctive need to check her image a moment ago, when she'd found him staring at her, no. Although she considered herself neither vain nor insecure, her psyche rebelled at letting any attractive man see her at a disadvantage. It was a power thing, a way to level the field, so that whatever the game, she could play with confidence. But the whole point of Friendship was not having to play games, to be able to feel safe in lowering her defenses.

Max waited, watching Sarina just sit there holding that creamer in midair. *Poor baby,* he thought. She's lost her concentration and fallen into some kind of catatonic state, just as she had that day in her office. She hadn't started playing with unlit cigarettes yet, but she was obviously nervous, stressed-out. He understood the pressures of her job all too well and really would love to help her ease them. If only he could dismiss the impression that the sparks he'd felt fly when they'd both reached for her purse hadn't been generated by him alone. That a very potent and potentially explosive sexual chemistry really did exist between Sarina and him.

The situation was looking bad. He had to snap Sarina back to reality and get her to stamp him a reject. Of course, Tony would only try to find another female client to take her place, but Max wasn't worried. Tony would never find another Sarina Mann. She was a one-of-a-kind woman—smart, classy, sexy. And the kind who really needed him. The kind he'd hate himself for walking out on.

So, he'd better walk while he could without regret. "Sarina," he began, gently flicking his fingers before her blank stare, "if you want to send me back to the agency because of my inexperience, I understand perfectly."

Seeing Max's eyes, Sarina remembered her coffee. She poured in cream, stirred, and took a sip, thinking that she wanted to send Max back all right, but not because of inexperience. She was afraid he had too much experience, the wrong kind. Setting down her cup, she said, "But you might lose your job. I'd feel awful about that."

Of all the things she might have said, Max hadn't expected her to say that. By the time many executives reached the heights Sarina had, they had fought so many battles for survival that they'd become deadened to the concerns of others. They couldn't afford the luxury. Max was touched, surprisingly and deeply touched. But he was in a battle for survival of his own.

"Don't worry, I won't lose my job," he said, unable to keep from laying his hand over hers to express his tender feelings. This time, again to his surprise, the resulting charge went to his heart instead of to the usual organ. Either way, it was a warning. "I'm part owner of the agency. So, your rejection can't get me fired. If you'd rather have a more experienced Friend, all you have to do is say so." Please say so, Sarina, Max pleaded as he lifted her hand and lightly held the pads of her fingers atop his.

Sarina looked at Max's fingertips supporting hers and wondered what kind of gesture he had meant it to be. Was it merely a metaphor for his support for whatever she decided to do? But there was also a courtliness about it, an expression of the regard of a knight for his lady fair. Had Max meant to comfort or court? Or arouse? She was so thoroughly confused, her pulse hadn't even bothered to surge, as though it was telling her to get the facts and let it know, once and for all, whether she was dealing with Friend or Man.

So, why *didn't* she get the facts? she asked herself. Why didn't she just come out and ask Max Evangelist if he was gay? Placing both hands in her lap, she fixed him with a direct gaze. "Max, before I decide, there's something I'd like to ask you. You don't have to answer if you don't want to, but—"

Involuntarily, Max's gaze left Sarina's and traveled over her shoulder. It had been distracted by a man rising from a table, a man Max recognized and most definitely wanted to avoid. A man who had, when he worked with Max several years ago, blamed Max for the breakup of his marriage. He probably still did.

Not that Max had been to blame. The guy had simply driven his wife, who worked in the same department with Max and her husband, so crazy with his jealousy that she finally told him what he wanted to hear. Unfortunately, what he wanted to hear was that she'd been having a torrid love affair with Max. During the bitter divorce that followed, recriminations between husband and wife shot through the department like bullets. As if turning the workplace into a war zone weren't bad enough, the husband went berserk on Max, sabotaging his computer files, shredding his reports, canceling his travel arrangements so that Max would get to the airport only to find his seat had been sold out from under him. If Max hadn't left to start Friends in High Places, the guy would eventually have forced him to do something he wouldn't have regretted in the least. Still, he didn't want to be forced to do it now, in front of Sarina.

Seeing the man walk toward them, Max lowered his head, shielding his face behind his right hand. He turned slightly to his left. He felt bad about appearing to be rude to Sarina, but he couldn't risk the guy's spotting him. Of course, if Sarina got the idea he was sleazy enough to seduce a co-worker's wife, she'd have no compunction about sending him back to Friends in High Places. On the other hand, he didn't want to give the agency a bad name.

Observing Max's rudeness, Sarina took instant offense. But on second thought, she wondered if he had suspected what she had been about to ask him. Perhaps *she* had offended *him*. Or embarrassed him. *Now* what was she supposed to do? Sliding her hand across the table toward him, she said, "It's okay, Max. I won't ask. I don't need to know. It's really none of my business. I'm sorry if I upset you."

Confounded, Max peeked at her. "*What* are you talking about?"

"The reason why you won't look at me."

"The reason I'm not looking at *you* is because I don't want a certain other person to see me!"

Sarina looked around. "Who, Max?"

"Did you say 'Max'?" A short, balding man with a pasty complexion stopped beside Sarina. He leaned across the table, peering curiously at Max. "Why, Max Evangelist, it *is* you," he said.

With a look of profound displeasure, Max finally turned around and looked up at the man. "None other," he said, his tone anything but cordial.

The man gripped Max's shoulder. "Well, Max, getting on with your life, I see. I wish that were as easy for the rest of us as it apparently is for you." He glanced at Sarina. "Aren't you going to introduce me to your companion, Max?"

Max would as soon have introduced her to a boa constrictor. "Ms. Sarina Mann, Mike Preston."

Sarina extended her hand. "How do you—" *Mike? The* Mike? "—do."

Unable to bear the sight of Sarina's hand in Preston's, Max reached out and returned it to her. "Don't let us keep you, Mike. I'm sure you must be in a hurry to get back to the office.''

"Oh, I'm in no hurry, Max," Preston said, malice lurking behind his civil tone. "Besides, I'm sure Ms. Mann would like to hear our story."

Their story? *Yes, this man certainly could be* the *Mike,* Sarina thought. He even had a paunch. But did she really want to hear the details of his relationship with Max? Did Max want her to hear them? "Perhaps some other ti—''

"No time like the present," Preston said. He began rubbing Max's shoulder, but far from affectionately. "You see, Ms. Mann, Max and I were once colleagues. You might even say we were a team." He looked at Max. "Until Max sneaked behind my back with someone he shouldn't have. Isn't that so, Max?''

If Sarina still had any doubts that Mike Preston was *the* Mike, then she really was a master of denial. No doubts lingered, however, either about Mike or about Max Evangelist, who, as Jack would say, was definitely as gay as a lark. She took a moment to consider the implications, not the least of which was that—oh, happy day—her meddlesome subconscious had finally been wrong about something. More importantly, she could now feel safe in keeping Max as her Friend.

But how could she think only of herself when poor Max was so visibly miserable? Straight or gay, nobody wanted the kind of scene Mike Preston was causing. Looking everywhere but at Max, Sarina raised her cup to her lips.

Personally mortified and furious at the embarrassment Mike was obviously causing Sarina, Max had all he could do to keep from wringing the damn fool's neck. With great effort, he limited himself to knocking Mike's hand off his shoulder. Slowly getting to his feet, he glowered down at the slighter man. "It's over, Mike," he said, referring to the Prestons' marriage. "It's about time you learn to live with it.''

Now that's a class act, Sarina mused. Unlike Rance, Max had had the decency not to resort to "It was bigger than the both of us."

"I am living with it, Max," Mike Preston replied. "I just want to be sure you never forget me and what you did to my life."

"There's nothing *to* forget," Max shot back. "Now if you don't get out of here by the time I count three, I'll throw you out on that thick skull of yours. One, two—"

Nodding at Sarina, Preston left the restaurant.

"I apologize, Sarina," Max said, sitting down. "The guy's a nutcase. It's no wonder that relationship fell apart. But I want you to believe me when I say that his suspicions about a love triangle were completely unfounded." Max replaced his napkin on his lap. "I'm no saint, Sarina, but I'm just not capable of that kind of thing. All that keeping track of lies...I have better things to do with my time. Besides, when I realize I'm losing interest in a person, I feel it's kinder to just be honest and say so."

"I couldn't agree more," Sarina said, wishing Rance had been half the man Max was. A wrinkle furrowed her forehead as she pondered the irony of that wish, but only fleetingly. The most important thing at the moment was to reassure Max. She took his hand, as she now knew he had taken hers earlier, in a show of support. "I believe you, Max."

Max looked at Sarina's lovely, slender fingers curled around his, then raised his gaze to hers. Was she just being kind, or was there more in her touch? He had to find out. Although he'd never see her again after today, at least he could dream of what might have been. "Sarina, before we were interrupted, what was it you were about to ask me?"

Sarina smiled sweetly. *I don't have to ask that now, Max.* "Whether or not you're free to go shopping with me tomorrow."

Max bolted upright, looking at her from the corners of

his eyes. "Does this by any chance mean we're Friends again?"

"Friends, pals, best buds." Sarina dug heartily into the salad the waiter set before her. "We'll be inseparable. That reminds me, you'll need a pager." Holding her fork aloft, she gazed across the table, knowing she must look as moony as Doris Day but not caring. "Oh, Max, you and I are going to make fantastic Friends."

His appetite gone, Max waved away the waiter who started to serve him his salad. He propped his chin in the palm of his hand, glumly aware that having found a new best Friend, he looked the way most people do when they've lost theirs.

"Yeah," he said, sighing. "Unbelievable."

4

"MAX, WHY ARE *you* asking *my* advice about women?"
Father Nick DeGrasso, his athletic shoes squeaking against
the floor of the racquetball court in the midtown gym, back-
handed a return shot. "That's like asking a vegetarian
where to get a good steak."

Max barely answered the priest's sizzling return.
"Yeah," he said, groaning, "but vegetarians aren't im-
mune to advertising and neither are you."

Grinning, Father DeGrasso made light work of counter-
ing Max's shot. "Maybe so, but give me a break. If you
want to discuss how many angels can fit on the head of a
pin or why you haven't been to mass since your sister's
wedding, I can hold my own. But when it comes to women,
I'll humbly concede to your expertise."

"And I'll concede this game, Nick," Max said, missing
his shot and slamming into the side wall. Pressing his back
to it, he slid to the floor and stretched his legs in front of
him. "I just haven't got the stuff tonight."

"I did notice you weren't exactly in top form," Father
Nick replied, propping his hands on his knees. He remained
bent over, slowing down his breathing. After a moment, he
peered at Max from beneath a wet brow. "If you don't
mind my saying so, pal, you look like hell."

"I haven't been sleeping well," Max replied, flexing his
knees and pushing off the floor. He ambled to the back of
the court, slipped his racquet inside its case, then took a
towel from his gym bag. After wiping rivulets of sweat

from his face, he turned to the priest. "I've been trying to tell you, Nick, I've got serious woman trouble."

Nick DeGrasso, black-haired, blue-eyed handsome, and with a physique that reflected the hours he spent in the gym each week, nevertheless regarded Max with deeply spiritual concern. "I see," he said, his tone reflecting the gravity of Max's problem. "And you don't want to marry her, is that right?"

"Of course I don't *want* to marry her. You know how I feel about the state of holy matrimony. It's not on my map." Hooking his towel around his neck, Max leaned over and grabbed the handles of his gym bag. "But I have to admit," he began as he stood upright, "I feel differently about this woman than I ever have about any other. It's crazy, but I almost feel responsible for her."

"I should hope you would," the muscular clergyman shot back in an equally muscular voice as he hoisted his own bag over his shoulder.

Max gave the priest a perplexed look. "Yeah, right," he said as he walked to the door, holding it for Father Nick then following him to the men's locker room. "Anyway, as I was about to say, it's way too soon to be thinking about marrying this woman." He laughed. "As a matter of fact, I haven't gotten much past cavorting with her."

Catching his companion by the arm, the priest whipped Max around to face him. "You may not have gotten past the frolicking stage, Max, but I can assure you, nature has. It's not going to wait for you to make up your mind about marrying this woman. It has a mind of its own."

"Are you ever right about that," Max replied, holding open the door to the locker room. He followed the priest to their lockers, opened his, then, sitting astride a bench, lifted one foot onto it and began unlacing his shoe. "Nature is precisely what I'm talking about. I need to know what to do about it." Lifting his other foot, he paused. "This whole situation is so delicate. I need to know how to handle it.''

Poking his head around his locker door, Nick DeGrasso looked down at Max, his gaze a mixture of alarm and disbelief. ''Max, think. Think of what you're saying.'' Reaching forward, he clamped a powerful yet ministering grip on Max's shoulder. ''I know three couples in my parish right now who are desperate for a baby and would give yours a fine, loving home.''

At last seeing the light, Max threw his leg over the bench and shot to his feet. His eyes bugged out at the priest. ''You mean all this time you were thinking I'd made some woman pregnant and didn't want to take responsibility for her and the baby?'' That the man he'd played racquetball with once a week for over two years, a man with whom he'd shared views on everything from religion to politics to sports, could believe him capable of such cowardice really hurt. Turning away, he flung his towel on the bench, took a deep breath, then confronted the priest. ''Come on, Nick. You know me better than that.''

''I thought I did, Max.'' Slowly, Father Nick sat down. ''So, there *is* no baby?''

Returning to his locker, Max removed his wet shirt. ''Not that I know of. At least, none belonging to me.''

''Thank God,'' the priest said, releasing a sigh. Rising, he removed his toiletries from his locker, glancing at Max as he did so. ''I was getting ready to beat the hell out of you, and believe me, I wasn't looking forward to it. Even on one of your bad days, you're tough competition.'' Closing his locker door, he extended his hand. ''I'm truly sorry, Max.''

Chuckling, Max rose and shook the priest's hand. ''It's okay, Father. I forgive you. But for half your penance, you'll have to buy drinks tonight.''

''Only if you promise to tell me about this woman trouble of yours.''

"Don't worry," Max said, calling over his shoulder on his way to the showers. "That's the other half of your penance."

Twenty minutes later, the two men sat opposite each other in a booth at a nearby grill, drinking hot chocolate. Father DeGrasso, now wearing his collar, set his mug down and looked across the table. "You know, Max, when a man tells me he has serious woman trouble, he usually means one of a few things. Since we're not talking about an unwanted pregnancy here, and *you're* not married, that must mean the lady is married."

Max sipped his hot chocolate, shuddering as it singed the tip of his tongue. He swallowed the "dammit" that leapt from his throat in deference to the Roman collar. "Nick, if I've avoided a marriage of my own this long, what makes you think I'd want to mess with somebody else's? No, she's not married, though she did mention she's seeing someone." Max frowned. The thought that Sarina might at this very moment be in another man's arms disturbed him far more than it should, or than he wanted it to. And far more than he could afford it to. "But that's not what I wanted to ask your advice about."

Nick DeGrasso made a wincing face. "Are you sure you don't want to discuss how many angels can fit on the head of a pin?"

"Some other time," Max said, his wry smile quickly fading. "I'm really struggling, Nick. You're the only person I know who can help me."

The priest rested his strong hands on the table. "Of course, I'll do what I can, Max."

Sitting forward, Max warmed his hands on his mug. "Nick, you're a good-looking guy—"

"Is this a proposition?" The priest waggled his eyebrows like Groucho Marx. "Sorry, Max. Go on."

Max ran his finger around the rim of his mug. "What I mean is, you're the kind of guy women are attracted to, and I know you don't always wear that collar. You can't tell me they don't occasionally come on to you.''

Scratching his temple, Nick DeGrasso cleared his throat. "Believe it or not, Max, sometimes they do even when I'm wearing the collar. I mean, it's not like women react to it the way vampires react to the sight of a crucifix.'' After giving a chuckle, he took a deep breath and released it. "Actually, I've had to work at keeping my vow of celibacy. And I can tell you, it hasn't always been easy.''

"But you've kept it," Max said.

Father DeGrasso rapped his knuckles on the table. "So far. Even so, I don't take anything for granted. I don't think that just because I've resisted temptation in the past I automatically will in the future. Collar or no collar, I'm just a man.''

"Exactly!'' Catching a few stares, Max lowered his voice. "You're a real man living in the real world, not in some monastery. You work with women, you counsel them. I assume you befriend them. What I want to know is, how do you keep yourself on the straight and narrow?''

"You mean, how do I think only pure thoughts?''

Max nodded.

The priest looked from side to side, as if making sure there were no eavesdroppers. He leaned closer to Max and spoke in a whisper. "I don't.''

Max's shoulders slumped, as if he were a balloon and the priest had stuck a pin in him. "I was afraid you were going to say that.''

"I'm not saying I invite sexual thoughts, Max,'' Nick said. "But when they occur, I don't allow them to become X-rated features.''

Max sat up, his gaze hopeful and intent. "Okay, so you're saying that aside from living in a cold shower, there are things you do to keep from thinking of a woman that way.''

The priest looked at Max from the corners of his eyes.

"Max, don't tell me you're thinking of taking the collar yourself?"

Max laughed with a snort. "No, Nick. I don't think I'm man enough."

"You're man enough. I'm just not sure you're a good enough racquetball player."

Max held his mug away from his mouth. "Say again?"

The priest shifted, stretching his arm along the back of the booth. "That's what I do in lieu of cold showers, Max. Sports, physical conditioning. Satan's no slouch, you know."

"In other words, healthy body, healthy mind."

"That—" Nick lifted his mug "—and sheer exhaustion."

The two men laughed.

Max began accordion-pleating his napkin. "Yeah, but what do you do when you're actually with a woman you're attracted to and there isn't a gym handy?"

Nick rubbed his chin, narrowing the cleft of it. "I guess I move around a lot. You know, keep from getting a visual lock on her. And I pray." The priest's gaze lighted on a tall blonde giving Max the eye as she passed, then again on Max. "But you know, the hardest part about being celibate isn't the lack of sex."

Max peered at his priest friend as though he'd just said the pope wasn't Catholic. "I suppose that's easy for you to say, but forgive me for being skeptical."

Nick drained his mug, setting it aside with a look at Max that was only slightly more understanding than amused. "Nevertheless, it's true." He gazed into the distance. "I think the hardest part of being a priest, for me, comes at the end of a long day of visiting twelve-year-old kids in alcohol rehab, and praying with an old widower whose only daughter doesn't care if he's dead or alive, and trying to help a young woman to believe that some good will come from her husband and her best friend running off with each other on her wedding night.''

"No kidding," Max said, looking up from the napkin he was now pleating at the short end. "Did that really happen?"

Nick nodded. "The woman is a real doll, too. Smart, funny." He faced Nick squarely. "You know, I ought to introduce the two of you. You'd make a great couple."

"Thanks, but no thanks," Max replied, waving his hands and thinking the woman couldn't be too much of a doll if her groom left her on their wedding night. "Besides, I have more than I can handle at the moment, remember?" He leaned forward. "Now come on, you were telling me about what it's like at the end of a long day of trying to help people—"

"Oh, right," Nick said. Propping his elbow on the table, he cupped his chin. "Well, the hard part is coming home feeling like you've failed, asking yourself why God ever picked someone as inadequate as you to do His work—and having no one to argue with you." He sat back. "That's when I wish I had a woman to come home to. A wife, a lover. A friend."

Max looked at the priest, but he was seeing Sarina, imagining what she might be like to come home to. Her sapphire eyes sparkled with wit, her smile dazzled him with the promise of—what? Things he'd never experienced before with any other woman. Perhaps, even friendship. "Nick, do you really think men and women can be both friends and lovers?"

Father Nick half smiled. "I know so. I wasn't always a priest, Max."

Max paused, appreciating the priest's candor. "But can they be *just* friends?"

"Sure," the priest replied. "Oh, I suppose they first have to deal with the question of whether or not they could ever be lovers, but often, that takes mere seconds. Still, they feel this bond between them. So, they rule out sex and fall deeply and eternally in like, instead.''

Max considered what the priest had said, then asked, ''Are you deeply and eternally in like with a woman?''

''As a matter of fact, I am. She and her husband moved to Florida some years ago. We don't talk as often as we used to. Still, there are times in each of our lives when no friend but the other will do, and we both know all we have to do is pick up the phone.'' Sitting forward, Nick pinned Max with a probing look. ''Max, this woman you were telling me about, I gather you're contemplating friendship with her?''

One side of Max's mouth quirked. Pushing the napkin aside, he leaned back with a sigh. ''I've already committed to it.'' Briefly, he explained the terms of his bet with Tony. ''As you can see, everything I care about in the world is riding on my ability to keep my relationship with this woman strictly platonic. The problem is, whenever I think about her, which is about every thirty seconds, she doesn't exactly bring Plato to mind.''

''In that case,'' Father Nick said, glancing at the waitress tallying their bill. ''You'll be wanting to play racquetball twice a week from now on.''

When the waitress deposited the check in the center of the table, each of the men grabbed a corner of it. They locked gazes. Max spoke first.

''Would you mind telling me how racquetball figures into this discussion?''

''Whoever this woman is,'' Nick said, ''she must be special.''

''Very,'' Max replied, finally wresting the bill from the priest. ''But why should that make me want to play more racquetball?''

Nick slipped on his jacket. ''If I'm not mistaken, you're restricted to friendship with her, but for some reason you're unable to pursue other women. She's got a hold on you, boy.''

Max reached into his jacket pocket for his wallet. "You know what? You were right. You were the last person I should have asked for advice about women because you don't know what you're talking about.''

"Oh, really?'' Sliding from the booth, Nick DeGrasso pressed his palms on the table and looked closely at Max. "A beautiful blonde sashayed by here a moment ago. Max, the look she gave you could have burned asbestos. And you didn't even notice her.'' He stood upright. "That's why you'll be wanting to play more racquetball. I predict you'll lose, oh, about ten pounds before the relationship between you and this woman goes one way or the other.''

Tossing bills on the table, Max rose. "Nick?''

"Yes?''

"Leave the tip,'' Max said, then walked to the door.

Chuckling, the priest left a dollar and change, then followed Max outside. "I'll call the gym and book the court for an additional night next week,'' he said, zipping up his jacket. "Tuesday, okay?''

Max agreed, wondering whether or not he'd have to have his suits altered to accommodate a loss of ten pounds. As he turned to head in the opposite direction from the priest, he paused. "By the way, how many angels *can* fit on the head of a pin?''

"Now that's a highly theological debate,'' the priest called as he walked backward. "Come to mass sometime and we'll discuss it afterward. If you're not too tired, that is.''

Waving to Nick as he headed for the subway, Max realized he'd just spent the last hour finding out what he already knew. He was going to love being Friends with Sarina—if it didn't kill him first.

IN HER OFFICE the day after her lunch with Max, Sarina waited on hold for Dr. Barrett Brown. As she did, she scanned the latest figures on the hotel in Rome she was considering acquiring for Global Century's small but growing fleet of luxury hotels around the world. On paper, it looked like a sound investment. But only an on-site inspection would tell the whole story. She was scheduled to leave for Rome in ten days, which left her more than enough time to prepare for the trip. The question was, should she ask Max to join her? After all, according to mythology, Rome was founded by the twin sons of Mars, Romulus and Remus, as though it were always meant to be shared.

Of course, Romulus later killed his brother. But Sarina remembered enough of her long-ago summer in his namesake city to know that she couldn't tread the ancient stones of the Forum, or stand before the *Pietà* in St. Peter's Basilica, or be serenaded at Ristorante Sabatini without instantly needing to proclaim her enchantment. How could she be a credible ambassador of U.S. business interests if she walked around Rome talking to herself? On the other hand, how would her Roman counterparts react to her traveling with a man who was neither her husband nor a Global Century employee?

Activating her speakerphone, she ambled to her window, trying to imagine how she would explain Max to the amorous Italians. "He's just my Friend," she whispered, instantly picturing the skeptical lift of an elegant Roman eyebrow. Gazing up, she clasped her hands behind her back. "He's *just* my Friend." No, that wouldn't work, she thought, pressing her middle two fingertips to her forehead. It sounded so defensive, they'd be certain Max was her lover.

Not that they were a people given to sniffing at such arrangements. In fact, that was the problem. When an Italian is in the throes of love, Rome could burn and he'd simply continue fiddling around. The group negotiating for the sellers would assume she was too enraptured by Max to notice they were taking advantage of her. She wouldn't allow that, of course, but clinching the deal could easily take twice as long as necessary. Her expense budget was generous, but not that generous.

But how she hated the thought of strolling the Via Veneto alone, without anyone to keep her from remembering that the last time she'd walked that romantic, tree-shaded avenue she'd been with Giorgio. The almost-lover who had propositioned her best friend Jillian. The ex-best friend who, years later, betrayed her with her husband on her hexed wedding night.

Sarina returned to her desk, running her finger down the report but calculating nothing. There had to be a way to bring Max along on her trip without ending up in a gossip column in *La Stampa*, she thought. She just needed time to find it.

"This is Dr. Barrett Brown."

Hearing her speakerphone blare, Sarina lifted the receiver to her right ear. "Doctor? This is Sarina Mann. I have good news." Succinctly, Sarina explained that she'd taken the therapist's advice, hired a professional friend and was now cured of her insomnia. She wasn't even packing a pack of cigarettes anymore. "I'd say you were a genius, Doctor," she concluded, laughing, "if you hadn't done yourself out of a patient."

"I'm delighted for you, naturally," Dr. Barrett Brown replied, sounding even more clinical over the phone than she did in person. "But I urge you not to assume too much too quickly. A brief respite from your insomnia doesn't necessarily indicate that the root cause of it has been eradicated."

Sarina tugged her left earlobe. "But you said the root cause was loneliness. Well, now, thanks to my Friend I don't feel quite so alone, and obviously, that's why I'm sleeping."

"Sarina," the doctor persisted, "I suggested you hire a Friend not as a cure for the underlying cause of your anxiety, but merely as an aspirin, if you will. Something to ease the pain while you work on healing your psychic wounds."

Sarina plunked into her chair. "Doctor, why is it every time we talk I feel worse than I did before we started?"

"That's my job, Sarina," the doctor replied, "to help you take an honest look at all those hidden owies your conscious mind would just as soon ignore."

Owies? Poor Julia, Sarina thought. She definitely had a major one that only a baby would heal. "But I don't have any hidden ow—psychic wounds."

"Have you been able to cry yet?"

Sarina recalled the tears that sprang to her eyes when she thought she might never see Max again. And how she'd convinced herself that they had arisen in response to a brutal wind and not a wellspring of emotion that Max had tapped into. Finally, she thought of how she'd so expertly forced them to retreat. And with good reason. Allowing her emotions free rein made her weak, vulnerable to the likes of Giorgio and Jillian and Rance. She'd been made a fool of for the last time the night she'd thrown the latter two out of her honeymoon suite. The same night she'd sensibly closed her life to future friends and lovers, vowing never to cry again.

"Frankly, Doctor, I don't see why you're so determined that I cry, as if they give medals for it."

"In a way, there are rewards for tears," the doctor said. "Crying cleanses the heart, Sarina. We all need to cry once in a while to make room for fresh emotion. This new hired Friend of yours allows you to satisfy some of your social needs without demanding very much of you in return. But you won't truly be able to move on with your life and establish mutually satisfying relationships until you come to grips with Rance and Jillian's betrayal, clean it out of your heart and make room for new feelings."

Clutching the phone cord, Sarina made a perturbed face. "But I *have* come to grips with what they did."

"I'm sure your mind accepts the fact of their betrayal," the amplified voice resounded. "But on a subjective, personal and emotional level? You're resisting, Sarina. Simply put, in all my years of practice I don't think I've ever met anyone who does denial the way you do."

Sarina rolled her eyes. She'd certainly heard that before. "Look, I came to you in the first place because I couldn't sleep. Now, I *can* sleep, and in my book, that's a cure."

"Whether or not to continue therapy is your choice, Sarina," Dr. Barrett Brown said, adding that should Sarina ever need her, she should feel free to call.

Sarina thanked the therapist, though she doubted she'd need her again any time soon. As far as she was concerned, there were too many people running around spilling their psyches. It was obscene, this new national pastime—true confessions. One of her favorite T-shirts read Thank You For Not Sharing Your Feelings. What this society could use was restraint, dignity, polite but impersonal conversation and a healthy respect for privacy. What she could use was an evening dedicated to all of the above. What she could use was an evening with Max Evangelist.

"WHEEEEEE!" Flying across the ice near the tail of the "whip" Max had coaxed her into joining, the wind smacking her to life, Sarina shrieked with giddy exhilaration. She snapped a backward glance at him. "This is insane. I love it!"

And I love holding you this way, Max thought, his hands firmly spanning her waist. But then, he knew he'd love holding her any way at all, though undoubtedly some ways more than others. Obviously, when Father Nick suggested he keep moving whenever Sarina was near, he had meant *around* her, not behind her. Especially tonight, when she was wearing a pair of leggings that hugged every one of her luscious curves.

"I'm glad you're having a good time," he shouted back, leaning so far into the turn that if his left cheek got any closer to the ice, he wouldn't have to shave in the morning. But that prospect wasn't nearly as disturbing as the view he now had of Sarina's firm, round bottom. Nick had certainly given sound advice when he recommended avoiding a visual lock-on. The problem was, dancing his gaze around Sarina only confirmed that there was no part of her that didn't inflame his desire. Racquetball twice a week might not be enough. In fact, he'd be lucky to restrict his weight loss to just ten pounds.

Suddenly, Max felt the woman behind him lose her grip on his waist. Looking back, he saw she was on her feet but speeding out of control and too stiff with terror to put the brakes on. He didn't want to let go of Sarina, leaving her at the end of the line. But if somebody didn't stop that woman, she was going to hurt herself and others. Like the gaggle of toddlers she was headed for.

"I haven't gone skating in Rockefeller Center in years, Max," Sarina shouted, tightening her grip on the waist of the man in front of her. "Whatever made you think of it?"

No answer.

"Max?" Sarina looked over her shoulder. "Max!" As the whip cracked, she saw him dig in his blades and take Olympic-sized strides toward the lock-kneed woman bearing down on a bunch of kids like Tonya Harding on a bad PMS day. Skating alongside her, he snagged her arm and maneuvered her away from the children toward the edge of the rink. Then, using his own weight as a drag, he slowed her down, eventually bringing her to a safe stop.

"What a guy," Sarina said. Suddenly, she realized she was at the very tip of a whip that had reached a land speed record. Hooking her fingers inside the waistband of the pants worn by the man who skated between her and the emergency room, she clung to her lifeline. Unfortunately, that lifeline was made of elastic.

Just my luck to get in line behind a pair of baggy sweatpants! Preparing for the next breathtaking turn, she gripped the waistband more tightly. To her horror, it began expanding.

Hearing Sarina scream his name, Max skated back onto the ice, searching for her. She wasn't hard to find. She was bringing up the rear, or more precisely, taking it away as she trailed the whip, and not by a nose. She was clinging to some poor guy's sweatpants, creating a gap between them and him only the Queensboro Bridge could span. His blades cutting into the ice, Max sped toward her. "Hang on, Sarina! Don't let—"

For one terrifying moment, Max lost sight of her. And when the whip lashed around, he saw she was no longer at the end of it. Pulling up and puffing out blasts of air, he scanned the crowded rink. She simply wasn't there. Choosing a corner, he skated toward it and through a throng, glimpsed her white ski jacket and pink scarf.

"Thank God," he murmured, but too soon. Sarina was sprawled facedown on a bench. Arms limp, legs splayed, her whole body inert, lifeless.

"Please, God, no," he said, rushing toward her so frantically he nearly lost his own balance. If anything had happened to her, he'd never forgive himself. Going ice-skating had been his idea. So had latching on to that lethal whip. Sure, she'd been a good sport and gone along; she'd even claimed to be enjoying herself. But he never should have allowed a mite like her to do anything so dangerous. All because when she'd called him to ask if they could spend a quiet evening alone together, he'd panicked. He hadn't thought he was capable of doing that, at least not without wanting it to lead to more. But Sarina, sweet Sarina, shouldn't have to pay for his lack of self-control.

As Max skated nearer to her, he gleaned movement. It was slight, but a shuddering motion nonetheless. For a second, he felt relief. She was alive, she was conscious. She was crying! She must be in excruciating pain, he thought, every bone in her small body broken because he didn't know how to be anything but one kind of man with a woman.

"Sarina," he called softly, hovering over her, wanting to lift her by the shoulders but afraid of causing further injury. "Sarina, it's me, Max. Where does it hurt?"

"Everywhere," Sarina squeezed out. Then, slowly and with evident effort, she turned her body over. Max saw that she was shaking all right—with uncontrollable laughter. Using her elbows for leverage, she hoisted herself onto the bench. "I would have hung on if I hadn't been splitting a gut," she spat out through laugh spasms. Clutching an arm about her middle, she pointed to the whip and the man with the stretch model sweatpants. "He's not wearing..." She doubled over. "Underwear."

Sarina soon had Max joining her in laughter. "That was worth crashing into a bench for," she said, finally settling down to a few chuckles.

Grinning, Max removed one glove. Touching his fingertips to her cheek, he wiped the tears streaking it.

Sarina met his gaze and instantly fell captive to its warmth and tenderness, to his ministering touch. A sobering touch. Turning from Max, she removed her own glove, raised trembling fingers to her cheek and felt the unfamiliar wetness of her tears. She assured herself that she hadn't broken her vow never to cry again because when she'd made it, she hadn't meant to include tears of laughter. At the time, she hadn't thought she'd ever laugh again. Still, tears were tears. To spill a few of one kind was to invite a torrent of every kind. Hurriedly, she wiped away their traces.

But she couldn't explain away the mysterious connection

between them and Max. Was it just coincidence that in the last two days, when she'd felt a sadness that had made her teary-eyed and a tickle to her funny bone that had made her cry outright, she'd been near Max? He was only a hired Friend, she reminded herself. He wasn't supposed to make her actually feel things.

Max looked at his fingertips, still wet with Sarina's tears. *Odd,* he thought. The few times a woman had cried in his presence, it had been because he was ending the relationship. He'd always tried to break it off before she felt enough for him to cry, but two or three times, he'd misjudged. More than enough times to condition him to feel like a heel at the mere sight of female tears, even in movies. Meg Ryan's chin-quiver alone could tear his heart out.

But he'd never been with a woman who cried with laughter—pure, contagious, belly laughter. He remembered wondering what Sarina's laughter would sound like, and now he knew. The world. A whole new world.

Yeow. Could it be, Max wondered, that a man and a woman really could have fun together without having sex? Even become the best of friends? Was it possible that he was—how had Father Nick put it—falling deeply and eternally in like with Sarina?

Not only was it possible, he thought, it was surprisingly satisfying. Like finding the one-and-only sweet for a one-of-a-kind craving. He squeezed Sarina's hand. "Girlfriend," he began, liking the taste of that word, "you really scared the hell out of me. Are you sure you're all right?"

Feeling his skin warming hers, Sarina wondered if she dare allow herself even that much sensation. She knew that when you give a feeling an inch, it can take over your life. "I'm all right," she said, withdrawing her hand.

For heaven's sake, Sarina, would you be happier if you turned to stone? The man is only showing you polite concern. If that's something to be afraid of, then let's all crawl back in our caves.

Sarina certainly couldn't argue with her subconscious about that. Still, she sensed that what Max had expressed was more than generic human regard for her welfare. He'd made her feel too special to him, as though his relationship with her was different from any he might have with any other woman. It was hard for her to imagine how, though, since his interest in women could only be platonic. Bending over to loosen the top laces of her skate, she scolded herself for needing to know that no matter what she was to Max, there was no one else quite like her in his life.

"Let me do that," he said, crouching before her, lifting her boot onto his thigh, and feeling an adolescent rush of chivalrous emotion. *Here I go again,* he thought, *acting like a dumb kid.* Only this time, he felt far less embarrassed. Maybe he *should* go back and start over, learn about women all over again, and about different ways of being a man. Maybe Sarina could teach him.

"Max?"

He gazed up at her, actually finding the reddened tip of her nose cute.

"Why did you call me 'Girlfriend'?"

Setting her foot down, he lifted the other. "Did I?"

"Uh-huh."

"I guess I did at that," he replied, congratulating himself. He felt as though he'd been inducted into an exclusive club where sex wasn't the only activity, or even the primary one. Rising, he said, "Well, that's what you are, isn't it?"

Pressing her palms into the bench, Sarina gazed up at him. "Yes, but do you call anyone else that?"

Confusion flitted across Max's mind, furrowing his brow. Was she asking whether he had other women friends whom he addressed as "Girlfriend" or whether he had a love interest whom he could rightly call his girlfriend? At the very notion that she might mean the latter, his heart lurched. But before he let it soar, he reminded himself that he'd already told her he was "in a relationship."

Nick had been right. Sarina might hold him to Friendship, but her hold on him went far beyond that. And he wasn't thinking only of sex or even romance. He was thinking that what he was beginning to feel for Sarina could be big, maybe even bigger than himself. He'd seen and heard her cry with laughter, yes. But she was crying out with something else—what, he didn't know—and she was crying out to him. Not because of him, but *to* him. The question he now asked himself was if and when he did discover the source of her heartache, what would he do? Would he run?

Turning his head slightly to his left, Max saw a man kneeling and tying his laces. There was nothing odd in that, except that he was certain he'd seen the same man follow Sarina and him from the Four Seasons yesterday. No doubt, he was Tony's operative, hired to tail them and report back to Tony any signs of intimacy in their Friendship. In a way, he was grateful for the reminder that if he wanted to keep his business, should Sarina ever cry with anything *but* laughter, he *had* to run.

But what should he do now? Looking down at her, he perceived a hunger in her gaze and realized that for some reason, she needed to know that among his friendships with women, the one he had with her was unique. It was, of course, because he had no other friendships with women. But just how friendly with her did he dare appear to Tony's spy?

Making sure the operative was still within earshot, Max held his hands out to Sarina. "Ms. Mann, if you would prefer I not call anyone else 'Girlfriend,' I won't. You're the client."

Placing her hands in his, Sarina allowed him to pull her to her feet. "Is something wrong, Max? Why the sudden formality?"

"Just doing my job, ma'am," he replied. Then, turning

his back to the detective, he gave her fingers a squeeze. Lowering his voice, he said, "I mean, Girlfriend."

Whatever confusion Sarina had felt over Max's abrupt mood swings vanished with his smile, as golden with warmth as the Italian sun. Suddenly, her breath caught in reaction to the stirring of blatant sexual need. Although he could never fulfill that need, perhaps by arousing it in her he would awaken her to the possibility of finding satisfaction with another man.

Oh, Sarina, she thought, what have you gotten yourself into? And why are you wondering what the Italian word for 'Girlfriend' is and how Max would sound saying it?

"Max?" she said, stepping alongside him as they headed for hot cappuccino. "Would you happen to have a valid passport?"

5

"MAX, I'M GLAD you appreciate that Satan never sleeps. However, I do. It's three in the morning, my man."

Pacing his living room barefoot, in a pair of rumpled trousers and with his shirttail half out, Max heard Father DeGrasso yawn at the other end of the line. He felt bad about having awakened the priest, but also envied him the pleasure of a deep sleep to be awakened from. Since leaving Sarina outside her apartment building five hours ago, he'd taken enough melatonin to put him in hibernation, drunk enough warm milk to assure he'd never need a hip replacement, and played so much computer solitaire the games were beginning to repeat. None of which had summoned the sandman. He hadn't even nodded off at C-SPAN, whose talking heads still loomed large on the sixty-inch screen behind him.

"I'm sorry, Nick," he said, clicking through the channels as he resumed pacing. "I wouldn't have called unless I was desperate. I don't know what to do."

Father Nick groaned with grogginess. "Are we talking about the same woman you didn't know what to do about the other night?"

"I don't mean to sound flip," Max said, halting his channel search on a close-up of Susan Hayward, her lush red hair a gleaming mantrap. He lowered himself onto his coffee table. "But at the moment I can't think of any other women I haven't known what to do about."

"I slouch corrected," Father Nick said drowsily, the

sound of head-scratching coming from his end of the line. "What seems to be the problem now?"

Max crossed his legs atop the granite table, transfixed by the feisty actress on the screen as she sashayed away from Robert Mitchum and across his screen. No woman could mesmerize him with just her walk the way Susan Hayward could, except Sarina. "She wants me to go shopping with her on Saturday. Last night I called her 'Girlfriend' and I guess that gave her the idea I'd enjoy raiding Madison Avenue."

"Wow, Max, you must have done something really nasty to deserve that fate," the priest replied. "Still, I don't think there's anything in the catechism about shopping being the near occasion of sin, at least not the kind of sin you're worried about."

Max leaned closer, zooming in on the video image. Like Susan, Sarina was not to be trifled with, which naturally made him want to trifle with her all the more. "You don't understand, Nick. We're going shopping for her trip to Rome, the trip she wants me to go along on."

"Hey, maybe you can put in a good word for me with the boss while you're there."

Closing his eyes, Max pounded his forehead with the pommel of his fist. "Nick, Father, help me out here, okay? That advice you gave me about keeping moving when I'm with her doesn't work. Especially when I'm moving behind her on ice skates."

"Ple-e-e-ease, Max," the priest said, his baritone grim. "No details. Believe it or not, I'd like to go back to sleep after we hang up."

As Mitchum and Hayward clashed on screen, Max tried to remember the name of the flick. "Look, Father," he said, eyes still fixed on the steamy action. "Trying to be nothing more than a Friend to this woman for a few hours a week is hard enough, but every waking hour for three days? I don't think I can do it. Especially not in Italy. The whole country is the near occasion of sin!''

Max heard running water at the other end, then a clanging, like a teakettle against a faucet. "Do you have any choice about going, Max?"

Trying to coax the name of the movie from the tip of his tongue, Max wondered why he felt he had to remember it.

"Max?"

Max rubbed the back of his neck. "You can take my word for it, I have to go with her. It's in my—" Suddenly, his eyes widened, his breathing grew heavy. Mitchum was crushing Sarina in his arms. "Contract." Had he just thought *Sarina?* Lord, what is the name of the movie?

"We will return to *The Lusty Men* after these messages," answered the prerecorded voice. Max clicked off the set and stretched out on the table. "What am I going to do, Nick? I won't have you to play racquetball with."

"How's your *bocce?*"

Max had been right about the teakettle. It gave a shrill response to the priest's question, saving Max the trouble.

"Okay, Max, look," Father Nick said. "You're going to have to set the tone of conversation with this woman, keep it on a high intellectual plane. You're an educated man. Engage her in philosophical discussions, introduce spiritual matters. It's been my experience that nothing quashes romantic stirrings like pondering the meaning of life."

Max's free hand dangled limply over the edge of the table. "And if that doesn't work?"

"Say two prayers and call me in the morning." Nick DeGrasso issued a protracted yawn. "And Max? *Later* in the morning."

HER JACKET over her arm, Sarina browsed through Armani's spring collection, elegantly displayed throughout the first floor of the designer's five-story Madison Avenue boutique. She knew she could have closed her eyes, laid her finger on any item, and have chosen well. Using that method she could no doubt outfit herself in record time. But that wouldn't be *shopping*.

For the first time in nearly a year, she was looking forward to some serious shopping, and with her new Best Friend. She could hardly wait to begin the whole feminine ritual—grazing through the racks, lunching at the Russian Tea Room, analyzing relationships. Well, not the last, certainly. As she'd told Dr. Barrett Brown, she was through with relationships and analysis alike. But that could only ensure the complete success of today's excursion. With her new Best Friend, she would have all the companionship she desired without first having to reveal the most humiliating episodes in her life, the way women do in order to become best friends. Examining a chartreuse jacket she'd taken from a rack, she wondered if the threat of blackmail wasn't at the heart of female bonding. Thanks to her new Best Friend, she thought as she rehung the jacket and moved on, she'd never know. Her new Best Friend wasn't female, and he was coming through the door right now.

Max stepped in from the cold and looked quickly around him, not for Sarina but for the assurance that he'd shaken Tony's snoop. Seeing no sign of the round-faced little man, he heaved a sigh, then scanned the store for the other visage that had been haunting him, waking and sleeping—mostly waking—for nearly two weeks. Sarina's.

Women flitted among the displays, lighting here and there like butterflies on bright spring flowers. But he had no difficulty singling out Sarina, as though his vision was uniquely tuned to *her* spectrum of color, his motion detectors sensitive only to *her* walk, the slightest incline of *her* head, the upturning of *her* nose. As he neared her, her fragrance embraced him, as though she were wearing it for him alone. Taking a deep breath, he closed his eyes and replayed Father Nick's latest advice. "Right, got it," he murmured. "High intellectual plane."

"Max!"

Max opened his eyes to find Sarina undulating toward him, moving sinuously through the displays in buff leather pants and a short sweater that flashed skin as she moved. His intellect took a plane out of town.

"I'm so glad you're here," she said. He found her smile so sexy, he let her lead him by the hand to a rack like an adolescent to the back seat of a car. "What do you think of this blouse?" she asked, removing a luscious pink confection and holding it beneath her chin. "No, wait."

She handed her jacket and bag to Max. Stepping back, she flattened the blouse against her abdomen, serving her breasts up, Max thought, like two scoops of creamy strawberry ice cream. "Is it me?" she asked.

Her hair was fire, her eyes lightning, his blood hot lava. "It's you, Susan."

A crease formed between Sarina's eyes. *"Susan?"*

Max shook his head, a reaction to the slap he'd just rendered his poor, sick, sleepless psyche. "S-s-s-arina," he said, "of course." He gulped as she turned in place for him, presenting him with a three-hundred-and-sixty-degree view of soft, supple sexiness. Feeling like Father Nick's teakettle about to blow, he massaged his temple. "Sarina, did you know that the romance of the high plains is being quashed?"

"What?" Sarina stared at him, then shrugged. "I take it you're talking finance? I guess that's what comes with agribusiness." She gazed down at the blouse. "Well, do you think I should get it?"

Max barely saw or heard her. He was looking into space, biting his thumbnail. If Sarina had thought he was talking pork-belly futures, Nick's advice wasn't quite working.

"Max?" Sarina took her bag and jacket from him, drawing his attention back to her. "Should I get it?"

"Hmm? Get what?"

"The blouse, Max." Half-laughing, she *tsked* at him.

"Sure, if you like it. Look, Sarina," he said, following her to a mirror. "Have you ever stopped to think that life is like a prairie?" *Now what am I saying?* Max raked his fingers through his hair. He was back in that damn meadow again, cavorting with Sarina.

As she gaped at his reflection beside hers in the mirror, Sarina's brows nearly shot off her forehead. Apparently, Max had a lot to learn about shopping. He didn't know he was supposed to save this meaning-of-life chat for the mocha torte they would share after lunch. Turning toward him, she looked at the blouse's price tag. Holding it out for him to see, she pressed close to his side, the crown of her head snuggling beneath his chin. "You don't think it's too much?"

His eyes closing, Max came to a boil as her hair stroked the right side of his jaw.

"Max? The price." Sarina eyed him with concern.

"Uh, yes, no. Well, maybe it is too much," he said. Then, seeing doubt in her upturned gaze, "On the other hand..." Moving to his left, he jammed his hands into his jacket pockets, away from the occasion of heavenly sin.

Sarina followed him. "You don't think the color clashes with my hair?"

Max took a step back, crashing into a rack and nearly overturning it. "Your hair? No, your hair is glorious," he said, bending to retrieve a dress he'd knocked to the floor. Suddenly, he shot up, his eyes wide. "I mean the color of the blouse is just glorious with your hair."

Cocking her head in puzzlement, Sarina turned away to file through a selection of skirts for one to go with the blouse.

Taking his hands from his pockets, Max wrung them. He had to find a way to keep the conversation from focusing on clothes and his mind from focusing on the lack of them. Father Nick, he recalled, had also said he should talk about spiritual matters. The only problem was, he didn't know of any. He pressed his fingertips to his forehead, drawing out memories of every talk he'd ever had with the priest.

Sarina held a skirt up. "Do you think this will go with the blouse?"

Max lurched toward her. "Sarina, I was wondering..." What *was* he wondering?

Startled by his sudden movement, Sarina abruptly threw both blouse and skirt over the rack. Holding her hand over her heaving chest, she settled an apprehensive gaze on Max. His behavior this morning had been so extreme, she truly didn't know what to make of it. One minute he was shrinking away from her, the next he was charging her. Overpowering her, actually. She felt a dizzying flush of desire, not totally unexpected, but certainly inexplicable. Pressing cool fingers to the back of her hot neck, she said, "Yes, Max? What were you wondering?"

"I was w-w-w—" Max looked frantically around. He still had no idea what he was wondering, other than what her incredible tangerine lips would taste like. Then he spotted a jewelry case. "Sarina," he said, snapping her into tight focus. "What do you think of angel pins?"

"*Angel* pins?" Sarina paused, as though trying to follow the thread of Max's conversation and finding it badly frayed. Then, suddenly, she seemed to understand. "Oh, you mean as in jewelry." Her smile, Max saw, grew soft and winsome. "You'll probably think this is silly," she began, her usually throaty voice turning to an intimate murmur, "but every time I see one of those pins I think of that prayer I used to say every morning when I was a kid. How did it go? Angel of God, my Guardian Dear..."

As Sarina recited the prayer, Max saw himself standing where he'd stood the last time he'd heard it, beside his mother's hospital bed. He was twelve and she was dying. "Max, promise me you'll take care of your sister," Kathryn Evangelist was saying. She took her son's hand in her fevered ones. "And don't forget to pray to your angel every day. Promise me, Max.'' She began whispering the words and when her breath gave out, Max finished them for her.

"To light and guard, to rule and guide," he murmured in a duet with Sarina, realizing he hadn't uttered those words from the day his mother died to this. He remembered thinking in his child's mind that he'd die himself before asking protection from the careless creatures who had failed his mother. Swallowing a lump, he blinked back tears.

"Max?" Sarina reached out her hand, resting it lightly but steadily on his sleeve.

Hearing her soft but commanding voice, Max looked at her. Despite the moist glaze over his eyes, he saw her as clearly as he'd just seen himself on that long ago day. He saw real concern and compassion in her expression, the kind that would remain watchful after he assured her he was all right. He saw that she was courageous, the kind to take charge when she found someone in distress. He saw that beneath her hard Manhattan veneer was a woman who, when she made a commitment, held nothing of herself back. He saw how deeply she could be hurt.

And how profoundly she could heal. If he'd heard her faintly crying out to him before, he now knew something in him was crying out to her. Sarina was his link to the child so deeply wounded by his mother's death that he rejected attachments to all women but his sister. She was already his responsibility and that was the one thing he'd never had it in him to reject. That was why he had resisted ever feeling responsible for another woman. But Sarina was reversing all that. She was his passage to every good thing he might have been and still could be. She was taking him home.

"Max?" Sarina touched her fingertips to his cheek, sensing the contrast between the warmth of his skin and the abrasiveness of his beard. He was a man of contrasts, yet somewhere deep inside him was a closely guarded wholeness that gave meaning to them. But Sarina didn't want to think about meanings. Certainly, a meaningful friendship was the last thing she had bargained for. Yet, she couldn't bring herself to withdraw her fingers. Where her flesh met his, a synapse formed between their hearts and minds, though ironically, not between their bodies. That could never be.

Then Max took her hand from his cheek and brought it to his lips. She stood transfixed, watching him kiss each finger, one by one. Then his eyes sought hers. He bent toward her. His presence, his scent formed a shelter around her. His lips came nearer, nearer.

The nearer Max brought his lips to Sarina's, the stronger was his need to do so, as though all his life had been a prelude to this moment. His gaze held her mouth the way a man holds a baby, half in fear, half in awe. How else to hold a miracle? Now that he was too close to see that mouth, he brushed his lips past it and placed them softly but firmly on her cheek. He might never find out how many angels could sit on the head of a pin, he told himself, but he would never forget what if felt like to kiss one.

As Max's lips, filled with tenderness and regard, touched flesh and a heart that had long forgotten both, Sarina drew a breath. Max had given her all she had secretly asked of him: friendship without risk and now, affection without commitment. She would be foolish and ungrateful to feel sad that he could never give her more.

I guess I'm foolish and ungrateful, she told herself as she allowed a single tear to course down the cheek Max had kissed.

SARINA MIGHT BE taking him home, Max thought, but not without taking him to the edge of his endurance.

In Rome, in a quiet hotel on the Via Veneto, he glanced about the room he'd occupied the last two days. It was small, but elegantly appointed, bespeaking the culture and wealth of the family whose former villa it was. That lingering ambiance of private privilege was the hotel's major attraction, he had agreed when Sarina tested her negotiating strategy on him last night. But there were drawbacks, too, any one of them a potential deal-breaker if the Italians decided to hold unreasonably firm to their asking price. Still, Sarina wanted the place—for some reason, she wanted it bad. And for that reason alone, he wanted her to have it. She had everything going for her—sound financial reasoning, a set of creative solutions to offer in the face of Italian obstinacy, and most of all, sheer guts. Beyond that, he was dying to know if any man could sit in a room with her and not give her anything she asked for. Well, since he was attending the meeting in about twenty minutes, he thought, glancing at his watch, he'd find out.

Taking his suit coat from a chair by the window, he gazed down at the unhurried, tree-lined street below. The scene had become a familiar one, Italians making an art of walking and observing one another. Unlike New Yorkers, they sought eye contact. Men gazed appreciatively at women, as though it were their privilege and duty, and women accepted male homage as their due. Entire love affairs could unfold in the time it took two people to pass each other by. What went on between the sexes was one of the sacred mysteries of life here. The Italians knew that to vulgarize it was to render it undeserving of high pursuit.

Opening his door, he stared at the one directly across from his, the portal to his own increasingly sacred mystery and object of high pursuit. Sarina's door.

Yesterday in the Forum, when she had taken his joking dare to stand atop the empty pedestal where an ancient vestal virgin had once stood, he'd gazed up at her and realized he was no longer in a joking mood.

Taking the cigar he'd been smoking from his mouth, he murmured, "Take good care of her, you lucky Henry you."

"Cary Grant, *The Bishop's Wife,* 1947," Sarina had shot back, playing the movie trivia game they'd devised, each delighting in trying to stump the other. "But what made you think of that, Max?"

"Because he should be standing where I am now. At your feet."

She had swept a flaming wave from her eyes. "Who, Max?"

He'd spoken in a hush. "The man who loves you."

Sarina had laughed. "There's no man who loves me, Max."

You're wrong, he'd wanted to say, shout. His heart pounded with wild hope. "Then, you're not seeing anyone now?"

"I sure am." Jumping down, she removed from her purse one of the slender cigars he'd bought for her to try and which she liked, sparingly.

As Max lit it for her, his hope plummeted. "Who?"

"You. My Best Friend."

Yes, but will you ever allow me to be more? What would you say if I told you that I would consider it the greatest honor if you would permit me to carry you back to the hotel and make worshipful love to you?

"Sarina..." Max stopped from asking her out loud. The local gumshoe Tony had hired was lurking only a few feet away.

SARINA STOOD at her window, gazing down at the small, walled garden below her suite, awaiting Max's gentlemanly knock at her door. She should have been thinking of the spot as an amenity to attract discriminating guests. Instead, she saw it only as it would shortly be in spring—an idyllic setting for a romantic tryst, lush as Eden, yet intimate enough to encourage the slow, torturing delicacies of expert lovemaking. Seeing herself languishing beneath one of the lemon trees in Max's arms, she turned her back on the scene, real and imagined. The only torture she would ever suffer on Max's account was the knowledge that such an encounter could never be.

She wasn't thinking only of her unbidden and futile sexual desire for him. In the last weeks, they'd grown at ease with each other, so at ease she'd inadvertently blurted out the truth about there being no man who loved her. Of course, knowing he was gay, she had no reason for wanting him to think there was such a man. Yet, she hadn't revealed far less intimate information, the usual data new friends collect—birthdays, family, where she'd gone to school. Neither had Max. And still, they'd grown close. Mere facts, she supposed, hadn't seemed important compared to the joy of discovering that they loved the same books and music and old movies. They had rattled off dialogue from their favorite films, laughing at their bad imitations of bygone stars, then challenging each other to name the film and the year of its release. They had talked politics, art, finance, the stock market over the phone until one in the morning and still not run out of conversation. Max, especially, never tired. He'd said he'd never really talked with a woman before, at least not the way he talked with her, and he was beginning to realize what he'd been missing. Sarina had been gratified, but also saddened. There was at least one form of intercourse to which she would never introduce him.

"It's the Hex," she said aloud. Turning from the window, she gathered her attaché case. In twenty minutes, she would enter negotiations for this hotel—her hotel—poised to pull off a deal that would make her a legend at Global Century. But in years to come, whenever she'd return to this place and look back on today, she wouldn't recall her triumph. She'd gaze down on that secret lovers' garden and recall that on this day she'd realized, too late, that she'd fallen in love with her Best Friend.

"REMEMBER, MAX," Sarina said as they stood outside a venerable building in the Via del Corso in the heart of

Rome's business district. "I'll introduce you to Signor Agnelli and his team as my consultant, which is only the truth." She looked down, afraid that her gaze might betray the depth of her feelings for him. "I can't thank you enough for helping me map my strategy."

Oh, yes you can, Max wanted to say. *You can show me I'm more than a consultant to you, more than a Friend.* Instead, he replied, "The strategy was all yours, Girlfriend. I merely confirmed that it was brilliant."

Nevertheless, as he followed Sarina inside, knowing the risks she was about to take and that he could do nothing but give her moral support, he felt his stomach clench. Suddenly, he realized what he'd feel like following her into the delivery room. As if that weren't jarring enough—the thought of Sarina having his baby—he also felt a twinge of compassion for his conniving expectant brother-in-law.

"This is it. D day," Sarina said as they stepped into the elevator, which like most of the elevators in Italy, barely qualified as a closet. "Wish me luck."

Max turned to her. God, she was so beautiful, in every way. "You won't need it, but I'll be pulling for you anyway."

Facing Max, Sarina wanted to ask him to please hold her close, not because she was afraid, but because he was a part of what she was about to do. He was a part of her. But despite their growing intimacy as friends, touching was now completely taboo.

Just yesterday, in the Forum, after much bantering about her posing as the missing vestal virgin, she'd playfully sneaked behind him and wrapped her arms around his waist. As though she'd sent an electrical shock through him, he broke her hold and turned, checking to see if anyone had observed them. Perhaps that reaction had been a holdover from his relationship with the suspicious Mike Preston. But the more she thought about it, the less certain she was that she could go on feeling the way she did about him, only to have him treat her like a leper. Another sleepless night like the last one, and she'd have to give serious thought to ending their Friendship before it broke her heart. Before—

"Oh!" Sarina shrieked as the elevator lurched violently to a halt, knocking her off balance. She would have fallen if Max hadn't caught her in a steely embrace, lifting her off her feet and holding her tightly to him. Her arms around his neck, she clung to him, her cheek pressed to his. Her heart jackhammered, as much from sensing the length of Max's taut body along hers as from her near fall. Then she felt something as incredible as it was unmistakable. The throb of his manhood against her thigh.

Slowly, she brought her gaze to his and knew she hadn't been hallucinating. She could see the smoldering of desire, and the terror of it. And she could also see that he had no intention of putting her down. If unutterable confusion was an aphrodisiac, she would be climaxing this very instant. Instead, she was about to faint from insatiable lust.

"*Buon giorno,* Ms. Mann. We're so happy to—"

Still locked in Max's embrace, Sarina snapped her head toward the voice, only now aware the doors had opened at their floor. Standing outside was a distinguished man with a full head of wavy, silver hair and two very unastonished blue eyes. *Italians,* she thought. They've been around so long they think they've seen everything, and they probably have.

"Ms. Mann? I am Signor Agnelli, at your service." He made a very slight, very formal bow with a very slight, very informal smile on his lips. He stepped to one side, revealing the man who stood behind him. "Permit me to introduce my associate, Signor Gaspari."

Sarina gasped. "Giorgio!"

At last, Max set her down, and not gently. "Who's Giorgio?"

In a daze, Sarina stepped from the elevator. Funny, she thought, the last time that question popped up, she'd lost a friend and a husband. Now, the curse was out to finish what it had started. She was about to lose her hotel, her secret garden of impossible dreams. And maybe even her career.

"GENTLEMEN," Sarina said, after three hours of negotiations, "as we Americans say, you drive a hard bargain." She held her hands up in a gesture of accession. "I'm now prepared to meet your final price."

Max coughed, covering his mouth and a smile. *Whose* final price, Sarina? He wasn't the least surprised she had clinched the deal on her terms while allowing the Italians to think she had agreed to theirs. For the last three hours, he had watched her with both amazement and admiration as she displayed an aplomb and a masterly skill at negotiation he had rarely seen before. Her feat was all the more impressive when he considered how obviously shaken she'd been at the start of the meeting, after that scene in the elevator. Come to think of it, he was still pretty shaken about that himself. Moreover, she'd had to maintain her focus under the blatantly amorous stare of Giorgio Gaspari, whom she'd apparently known before. She handled him beautifully, though, looking directly at him but with no indication that she'd seen anything more significant than a common housefly. Not that that had kept Max from wanting to punch the two-bit Casanova's lights out.

The meeting ended, handshakes went around the small conference room. Max said nothing to Sarina until they exited the building. Taking her by the elbow, he turned her toward him, barely able to keep from picking her up and swinging her around. "Girlfriend, you were magnificent!"

"I agree, Signor Evangelista," another man said.

Turning, Sarina and Max watched Giorgio Gaspari approach.

"*Ma,* I knew she was *magnifica* a ver-r-r-ry long time

ago," he said, stepping directly between them. "Sar-r-r-i-na, may I speak to you, *privatamente, per-r-r favor-r-re.*"

The hair on the back of Max's neck stood on end. He tapped Gaspari on the shoulder, once and very hard. "*Signore,* let's you and I have a word first." Confirming he wasn't being observed by a Roman Sam Spade, he pulled the Italian aside so that Sarina wouldn't overhear. "Roll one more 'r' at her and the next one will be through a gap in your teeth. *Capisce?*"

With a sly smile, Gaspari nodded and returned to Sarina. "You are more beautiful than ever," he said, his dark gaze caressing her.

She smiled beneath an arched brow. "And you, more than ever, are full of...of...*garbaggia.*"

Gaspari's teeth flashed white against his trendy smudge of beard. "Your friend, what was her name?"

"Jillian?"

"She told you I asked her out."

"She did," Sarina said, adding for pride's sake that she hadn't been surprised.

Gaspari shrugged. "What can I say? I'm Italian. I suppose, now, I won't ask you to dine with me tonight."

Sarina snorted at the arrogance of the man. "I think I'll survive."

Gaspari glanced over his shoulder at Max. "Is for the best. Your *innamorato* would not like you to go with me."

"Max? My *beloved?*" Sarina inhaled sharply. "Giorgio, I thought I explained that scene in the elevator. Max had grabbed me only to keep me from falling."

Gaspari shook his head. "I do not base my judgment on the elevator alone. You see, I can feel his stare right now, like a knife at my back. He is watching to make certain I don't step on myself."

"Huh?" Sarina heaved a perturbed sigh. "You mean 'overstep yourself.' Anyway, you're imagining it, probably because you're used to being followed by jealous husbands."

"Perhaps is true," Gaspari said. "But Sarina, I have seen the way he looks at *you.*"

Sarina's jaw dropped. She blinked once before speaking. "I told you, Max is only my consultant."

He waved a finger. "No. He is more than that."

Sarina was beginning to find this conversation entirely too painful. Eager to end it, she gestured impatiently. "Well, yes, he's a dear friend. But believe me, that's all."

"Sarina, do you take me for a fool?" Gaspari shook his head scornfully. "As I said, I'm Italian. I know the way a man looks at a woman when he worships her, when he wants her for his own. And I say to you that for three hours, I have seen Max Evangelist look at you that way."

"But...but that's not possible," Sarina replied. Nevertheless, she rubbed the place on her thigh where she'd felt Max's arousal, the arousal she'd finally dismissed as a fluke, an involuntary sexual response to danger. Still, while she couldn't trust Giorgio as far as she could throw him across the Colosseum, he had no reason to lie to her about what he'd seen, or thought he'd seen. And he *was* Italian.

She clapped the palm of her hand against the side of her face. *"Mamma mia."*

6

THE DAY AFTER returning from Rome with Max, Sarina sat in Dr. Barrett Brown's office, in the Mother of All Chairs.

"Doctor, the reason I wanted to see you is that I'm confused about my Friend, M-m-m-" Recalling that the therapist had said she knew the owners of Friends in High Places, Sarina paused to consider just how well she knew them. Perhaps not well enough to know that Max was gay. If so, Sarina didn't want to out him. He might sue her. Worse, he'd hate her. "M-m-mister Stan" she said.

Dr. Barrett Brown peered over her glasses. "Mr. Stan?"

Sarina rolled her eyes. She'd grabbed her father's name out of thin air and made Max sound like a hairstylist who wore white socks. "The problem is," she quickly added, "I'm not at all sure he's what you're probably thinking he is." She recounted the reasons for her quandary about Max's sexuality, from Mike Preston to the elevator in Rome to Giorgio. Taking a cigar from her silver case, she began tossing it from hand to hand. "So, what I was wondering is, do gay men ever…switch sides?"

"Well…" Rising, Julia Barrett Brown walked to the print on the wall, the one Sarina had said looked like a uterus. Peering at it, she spoke absently. "They sometimes switch-hit. But change leagues? It's rare." She looked directly at Sarina. "There are some things not even the love of a good woman can, or perhaps should, change, Sarina."

Sarina put the cigar down. "Then, if I were to have any romantic feelings for Mr. Stan…"

"Then I'd say you ought to ask yourself *why* you have those feelings."

Sarina laughed. "That's no mystery. He's handsome, smart, funny. We talk for hours and he really listens to me. He's always there for me." She sat back, tucking one leg beneath her. "He really is my best friend."

"And he's gay." Dr. Barrett Brown returned to her seat. "He can never betray you sexually."

Sarina's braced her hands on the arms of the chair. "Are you saying that I deliberately chose to become romantically attached to a gay man because, on a subconscious level, I knew he could never hurt me the way Rance did?"

"Did you?"

Sarina picked up the cigar, flexing it until it broke. "I don't know. I just don't know. But if I did..." She drew up the other leg and curled into the fetal position. "If I'm ever going to move on from Rance and Jillian, I might have to lose a man and my best friend all over again. I might have to give up Mr. Stan."

MAX SAT in his office at Friends in High Places, staring at the phone as though it held the secrets of the universe. Actually, he wouldn't have cared if it had. All he wanted to know is why it hadn't brought Sarina's voice to him in over a week. On the flight home from Italy, she'd been reluctant to engage in conversation, not even in the banter that came so easily to them. He'd thought she was simply exhausted from the intensity of the negotiations, but she'd slept little during the trip. Several times, he'd awakened to find her staring at him, obviously perplexed. She would look into his eyes, then, shaking her head as if still confounded, look away.

At the time, he'd thought she might have been recalling how she'd aroused him in that elevator. Lord knew, sitting close to her on the plane, he'd been able to think of little else. Perhaps she'd been wondering if she should confront

him about it. If she had, he would have either denied it
happened, or apologized for it. Either way, he might have
set himself up for the harassment suit he'd warned Tony
about from the beginning, when he'd discovered the client
Tony had chosen for him was a woman. What worried him
now was that Sarina might have decided on a course of
action he'd find infinitely more painful than a lawsuit. She
might have simply decided never to see him again.

On the other hand, he thought, turning to look out his
window, what if something had happened to her? What if
she needed him and was too sick or hurt to call? He knew
it was against the rules for a Friend to initiate a call to a
client, but wasn't it only natural to worry about someone
you hadn't heard from in a week, someone you'd talked
with and laughed with and practically lived with? Someone
who'd brought tears to your eyes and made you want to be
a better man?

Striding to his desk, Max grabbed the phone and began
to dial Sarina's work number.

*Did you hear yourself just now, Max? Put a gray wig on
you and raise your voice two octaves and anyone would
think you were Sylvia Weinstein fretting over the welfare
of one of her clients.*

Slowly, Max replaced the receiver, then sat down, forced
to face a shocking truth. He'd done the very thing he required the Friends not do. The thing he'd been so certain
it was possible to keep from doing. He'd come to really
care about a client. Sarina was a unique client, to be sure.
A woman he worshiped and desired, a true friend who'd
helped him to discover things about himself he'd never
known. But he realized that even if he hadn't felt that way
about her, even if he hadn't particularly liked her, he still
would have wondered what had happened to a steady client
who had abruptly vanished. Wondered and worried.

Whoa. Was it possible that he'd been wrong about
Friend/client relationships? Anything was possible, he sup-

posed. But if he'd been wrong, then Tony was, by definition, right. What a revolting idea.

Still, no matter how much disgust he felt at the thought of Tony's having a point other than the one on his head, Max was determined to find out what had happened to Sarina. He dialed her number again, and again he stopped before completing the call. He wouldn't put it past Tony to have his phone tapped.

Perhaps it was just as well, he thought, returning to the window. He'd already admitted he might have been wrong about something and Tony right. That was trauma enough for one day. He didn't need to do the one thing he'd taken a sacred oath he'd never do again. After he'd given his sister away to another man to worry about, he'd vowed he'd never again feel responsible for a woman.

YOU MISS HIM, don't you, Sarina?

Lying in bed, Sarina stared at the ceiling. "I did what I had to do."

If you were so sure of that, we'd both be sleeping right now.

Sarina swung her legs over the side of the bed and glanced at her clock. It read 2:16. In the last week, her insomnia had returned with a vengeance, as if to make up for all the sleep she'd gotten prior to the Rome trip. She pulled down her lower lids, easing the discomfort of overworked, under-rested eyes. Slumping to the foot of the bed, she put on her robe, letting it hang unbelted as she stumbled to the kitchen. She took a mug from a cabinet, then leaned on the sink as she filled it from the hot-water dispenser.

"Dr. Barrett Brown thinks I'm right to end the relationship," she said, plunking a Sleepytime tea bag into the mug just for the heck of it. "Where did *you* get your degree?"

At the best school, from the best teacher. Your heart.

"My heart is on permanent sabbatical," Sarina replied. Disposing of the tea bag and randomly grabbing a bag of cookies from the pantry, she shuffled to the table and sat down. Reaching for a cookie, she looked at the bag and saw she'd selected chocolate amaretto. She shoved the package away, rejecting all things Italian. They only reminded her of Max.

Max in the elevator.

"Stop it! I can't stand you harping at me any more. Haven't I been through enough in the last year?" Pushing herself away from the table, Sarina wrapped herself in her arms, enjoying no comfort. *What a difference a year makes,* she thought, *or doesn't.* She was jolted by a sudden realization. Her voice quivered when she spoke. "Don't you know what today is?"

I know what today would have been. Yours and Rance's first wedding anniversary.

"Yes," Sarina whispered, leaning on the back of a chair. "And haven't I done a remarkable job of putting my life back together? A year ago I married a man I didn't truly love. Today, I truly love a man whose one and only sexual response to me was purely unintentional."

The important thing, Sarina—the really important thing—is that you do love him. You love him in every way there is to love a man, even if he hasn't fully reciprocated. I'd call that real progress. Don't worry. You'll get it right next time.

"There isn't going to be a next time! There isn't going to be another Max." Suddenly, Sarina began a quaking that started with her head trembling and ended in legs that refused to support her. She fell sideways in the chair, splaying her arms across the table. "Oh, dear God, how did I ever allow myself to get so all alone?" Clawing at the table, she continued to shiver. "How am I going to get through the rest of this night? If only I could cry. Finally, I want to cry and I can't."

She glanced toward her living room and the cabinet that concealed a bar she kept amply stocked for guests who never came. Using the table as a brace, she got to her feet. Walking to the bar, she stood before it in the dark. She reached for the pulls.

Call Max.

"I can't."

You said yourself he's your best friend.

"It's three in the morning."

It's your last chance. You can call Max now or call A.A. a year from now.

Sarina made her way back to the kitchen and dialed Max's pager number. "He won't call back, I know he won't," she said when she'd finished pacing and shaking. "Why should he? I left him at the airport with a lie. I told him I'd see him soon and then ended our Friendship without so much as a 'Thanks, it's been fun.' What a coward I am. What a—"

When the phone chirped, Sarina lunged for it. "Max? Oh, Max, I need you."

HEARING DESPERATION in Sarina's voice during their phone conversation, Max had sprung out of bed like the entire Red Cross responding to a disaster. He hadn't been able to get more out of her than that she needed him. But that was reason enough for him to tear around his apartment, washing and dressing in record time. Grabbing his coat and keys, he started out the door, then paused and glanced at the window overlooking the street below. He walked to it and drew the drape aside, careful to avoid being seen.

"Damn you, Tony," he muttered, spotting the car parked across the street and the figure inside it. He'd seen both parked there before, several times, since he'd returned from Rome. "Do you have to be both right *and* a pain in the ass?" With just two weeks until their bet would be off, Tony was pulling out all the stops trying to get proof that he and Sarina had become more than just friends.

Stepping away from the window, Max paced. He knew

the utility door downstairs was wired to a siren, eliminating that exit route. He could climb down the fire escape, but one of his neighbors was bound to hear him, shoot first and ask questions later. How the *hell* was he supposed to get out of the building without being detected? He plowed both hands through his hair, hearing the urgency in Sarina's voice and growing more desperate.

Snapping his fingers, he ran to his bedroom closet. Minutes later, he emerged from the back of it with all that remained of his near miss of a relationship with Camilla Price. After several more minutes, he checked himself in the mirror.

"A man's gotta do what a man's gotta do," he said, making his voice especially deep.

SARINA KNELT in front of the fireplace in her living room, lighting the gas log. She'd stopped trembling the instant Max had told her to hold tight, he'd be right over. But until he arrived, until she could warm herself under his gaze, she needed a substitute.

Leaning back against an ottoman, she stretched one leg before her and suddenly wondered if she shouldn't have taken that drink instead of calling Max, after all. In her despair, she'd forgotten what those eyes of his could do to her. How they could take her to fields of wildflowers and new innocence, and icy wonderlands where he tenderly wiped away the crystal tears of her own laughter. To retail palaces where the most precious item had been his kiss on her cheek. And to a secret Eden in Rome, redolent with lemon and the embraces of lovers, that she would never share with him.

You're not entirely sure of that, are you, Sarina? In spite of what Dr. Barrett Brown said, you keep wondering about that day in the Forum, when he quoted that line from The Bishop's Wife, *then asked if you were still seeing anyone.*

"Just don't start on me, okay!" Sarina hugged her knees. "I've had it with this Is-He-or-Isn't-He? business."

Hey, maybe his hairdresser knows for sure.

Sarina twined her arms. "Look, what is it going to take to convince you that Max is who he is and he's perfectly happy that way?"

Size 12 platform shoes?

"That does it!" Sarina clambered to her feet. "I'm going to do what I should have done a month ago. I'm going to come right out and ask him the minute he gets here. I won't even let him into my apartment until I know." Charging down the hall, she took the elevator to the first floor, muttering her impatience for Max to arrive and untangle her confusion once and for all.

At the entrance to her building, she paced before the door. When the buzzer announced a caller, she confirmed it was Max and buzzed him in. She stood back, squarely facing the door. As it opened, she raised a finger in the air.

"Max, there's something I have to—"

Sarina broke off, her breath snatched away by the sight of the woman standing before her. She was statuesque in a brown leather jacket and an ecru satin robe that barely reached the middle of her shapely—and hairy—lower legs. Her ankles bowed and her heels hung over the backs of satin mules. Sarina trailed her eyes upward—six feet, one inch upward—and saw that the woman had lustrous, long platinum hair. And a dark layer of stubble.

Sarina's arms plunged to her sides. She gave the woman another once-over, only then realizing that she'd been clinging to hope, from the look of things, by a string of faux pearls. "Oh, Max."

"Sarina, this isn't what you think," Max said, peering behind the door and at the street one last time to be sure he hadn't been followed. Still, he wasn't certain which was worse, having Tony catch him running to Sarina's aid in the middle of the night or having Sarina catch him in drag.

He'd planned to ditch Camilla's glad rags between the ground floor and Sarina's apartment, never imagining she'd meet him at the street entrance. Closing the door, he stepped into the foyer. "I know this looks strange—"

"It's okay, Max," she said, shoving her hands in the pockets of her jeans. "Friendship means never having to explain your wardrobe."

Max stepped toward her, holding a gold lamé clutch purse in both hands. "But I want to explain. I *have* to explain." *I can't explain without telling her that I'm being followed and why. Tony may be right, but he's going to have to prove it to win the bet. I'll be damned if I'll lose to him on a technicality.* "Only I can't right now. Just trust me, Sarina, please."

Sarina gazed into his eyes, wondering how to keep from looking for what would never be there and knowing that if she didn't want to give Max up entirely, she must. "I wouldn't have asked you to come if I didn't trust you," she said. Then, realizing she hadn't trusted anyone in a very long time, she smiled. "But if you don't mind my saying so, I don't think platinum is your shade."

Max chuckled. "I knew I could count on my best friend to be frank with me."

Sarina cocked her head to one side. "Am I your best friend, Max?"

Max folded his arms beneath the tea towels he'd use to create a bustline. "If you're not, what am I doing here in the middle of the night?"

"Looking for me, I hope." Jack, Sarina's neighbor, stood before the elevator's closing doors, cuddling a black cocker-spaniel puppy on a leash. He looked Max up and down, a suggestive glint in his gaze.

Propping one empty fist and one clutch bag on his waist, Max squared his shoulders at Jack. "I guess this just isn't your night, fella."

Sniffing, Jack tossed his scarf over his shoulder. "Pity," he said, and walked out the door.

After he'd gone, Sarina and Max pointed at each other. "Coral Browne, *Auntie Mame,* 1958!" They laughed over the line they agreed was the very definition of pith, then a moment later, grew quiet.

Max removed his wig. "You okay?" he asked, shedding the rest of his getup. "You sounded really awful on the phone. I got here as fast as I could."

Obviously, Sarina thought, slightly embarrassed but also fascinated to watch him change—not just clothes but personas. Now that she thought about it, the more she saw of his alter ego the easier it might be for her to get over her romantic delusions about him. She'd already forgotten that in the back of her mind, she'd been hoping the elevator would give them a jolt. "I'm sorry you rushed," she said, stepping inside it. "I should have made it clear I wasn't sick or hurt."

In her faded jeans and soft-pink, ribbed knit shirt, she looked like the gamine of his dreams. Sarina obviously wasn't sick, Max thought as he followed her. *Thank God.* But noticing the roil of emotions making her blue lagoon eyes murky, he was sure she was hurt. "No need to apologize, Girlfriend," he said, stooping to roll down the legs of his slacks.

Sarina gazed down at his shoulders and his broad back. They may have recently been clad in satin, she thought, but they were strong. Strong enough to get her through the night. Perhaps through a good deal more.

Smoothing the fabric of his slacks, Max noticed that Sarina was barefoot. They were small, her feet, and tipped with polish the color of pink carnations. One poised precariously atop the instep of the other, its sweet toes grasping and mingling with the equally sweet ones below, like five lost souls searching for their mates. As he slowly straightened, the doors opened and he knew he was about to discover, at last, the hurt inside his best friend.

SARINA WALKED to where Max sat on the floor in front of her fireplace, carrying two mugs of instant hot chocolate with marshmallows. She handed one of the mugs to him, then sat beside him, her back next to his against the ottoman, their shoulders touching. "Max," she began, pausing to sip the frothy brew. "Has anyone ever hurt you so bad you couldn't admit it, not even to yourself?"

Max stared at the fire, seeing that twelve-year-old boy who had lost the first woman he loved, the boy Sarina had reintroduced him to with the words of a forgotten prayer. "Once. A long time ago."

Still gazing at the fire, Sarina cocked her head away from his. "What did it do to you? The denial, I mean."

Watching the blue-lined flames dance, Max drew up one knee. "For years, I thought it protected me from ever having to feel that kind of pain again." He sipped his drink, then slowly let out a breath. "Now I know that the only thing it protected me from was really loving and being loved in return."

Sarina gazed into her cup, marveling that a man whose orientation to life and love was so different from hers had so perfectly described her own response to emotional trauma. But then again, what was so surprising about that? He was, after all, her best friend. Curling her legs under her, she turned to him, propping her elbow on the ottoman and her chin on her fist. "So, how did you finally come to terms with it? The hurt, I mean."

Setting his mug aside, Max looked at her. With her hair a halo of firelight, he found he was unable to resist it. Gently, without touching her skin, he pushed a single ray from her brow. "With the help of an angel."

Sarina's eyes momentarily closed at his near touch. For

a moment, she thought she might cry, but the urge passed. She set her own mug aside. "Max, be an angel."

Several minutes later, after listening to Sarina's disjointed tale of marriage and mayhem as she paced the room, Max had to stop her. He rubbed his tired eyes with thumb and forefinger. "Now, if I understand you correctly, today would have been your first wedding anniversary had something called the Mann Hex not revived disco."

Interrupting her pacing, Sarina sighed. "Close enough."

"You're no longer married, then?"

"No longer than six hours."

Max gave a silent sigh of relief. Watching the walk that drove him and Robert Mitchum crazy, he asked the next most important question. "So, did you love this what's-his-name, Rancid?"

Sarina lodged a hand in her tousled hair. "Rance. And I thought I did, once. Now, I don't know how I ever could have. Believe me," she said, shooting him a glance, "he'd never have come running to my rescue in the middle of the night the way you did."

"Well, you know…" Max smiled modestly. Then, clearing his throat, he grew solemn. "You're well rid of him, Sarina."

"You can say that again. The things I could tell you about that man."

"Actually," Max said, catching her fragrance as she passed before him, "I was hoping to hear more about the invisible peignoir you bought."

Halting, Sarina looked down at him. "It wasn't actually invisible, Max. It was just very lacy. Besides…" She pointed at the chair where his own discarded boudoir attire lay. "This is no time to compare bargains." Feeling she hadn't been quite fair, she knelt before him. "Look, I know I haven't been making sense. I guess I'm trying to avoid admitting what I really felt that night."

"And what did you feel?" Max's voice made a cushion for her response.

"Humiliated." Taking a breath, she sat back on her heels and lowered her head. "And I can't seem to get over it."

Taking her chin in the crook of his hand, he lifted her downcast gaze to his. "Yes, you can, Sarina, and I'll be right beside you all the way. But first, will you do something for me?"

Sarina nodded.

"Will you let me hold you? Just one human being comforting another, of course." *I promise not to embarrass either of us the way I did in that elevator in Rome.*

Sarina's lips parted in surprise. "Do you really want to?"

"I'm not saying it will be easy," he said, with a sidelong smile. *In fact it will be damn near impossible to put my arms around you and think only platonic thoughts.* "But I'd like to try."

Gazing into his beautiful eyes, golden with sincerity, Sarina wondered how she could refuse his request. She'd taught him how to talk with a woman, perhaps now she could help him to be physically close to one without recoiling. "All right, Max."

Telling her to relax, he took her by the shoulders and turned her so that she sat between his outstretched legs, facing the fire. "It's okay, lean back," he murmured, gently pulling her against his solid chest, sensing her deep mistrust of men. Circling his arms about her, he held her only tightly enough to make her feel secure, then brought his lips to her ear. "Now watch the fire, Sarina, and just say what's in your heart."

Sarina laid her head back on Max's strong shoulder, then rested her hands atop his, clasped and forming a shelter around her. Feeling the hairs on the backs of them, she took courage, as though they were the visible signs of the strengthening bonds between her and her best friend. She began her story again, from the beginning.

Gazing past Sarina, feeling her hair against his cheek kindle a fire of protectiveness inside him, Max listened to her story of betrayal by her husband and a trusted friend on her wedding night. It sounded so like a soap opera, he could hardly believe it was true. Yet, he'd recently heard another true story just like it, though he couldn't remember from whom. Probably from his due-any-day sister, whose current emotional state made her gravitate toward tales with a high sob factor. He remembered thinking when he heard it that the woman must have been a loser for her husband to abandon her on their wedding night. But the woman in his arms, snuggled against his chest, was so far from that, he had to chide himself for that shallow and all-too-male reaction. Apparently, there were enough of a certain kind of man running around Manhattan to warrant resurrecting the term "cad." He'd certainly like to meet the cad who'd abandoned and humiliated Sarina—just once and in a dark alley.

"So, there I was," Sarina said, finishing her tale. "The proverbial unkissed bride. I felt so naked, Max, so rejected as a woman."

Max tilted his head onto hers. *That's one thing you never have to worry about. Well, maybe the naked part.* The smile in the corner of his mouth and the fantasy that had engendered it faded, however, as he understood at last that executive stress wasn't the reason Sarina had called on the services of Friends in High Places. With good reason, she trusted neither friendship with a woman nor commitment from a man. So, she'd sought someone who wouldn't betray her because he was being paid to be loyal. "Poor Girlfriend," he said, hugging her tighter.

Responding to his nickname for her and to his embrace, Sarina felt secure in finally confessing the whole truth. "Sometimes, I still do, feel inferior as a woman, I mean."

She had thought that when she'd finally found the mettle to speak the depth of her wound out loud, she'd also find release in tears. Instead, lying in the arms of her dearest friend, she felt remarkably serene.

Max inhaled deeply. Closing his eyes and making fists of his hands, he fought a deep and desperate need to show her just how womanly she was, how infinitely desirable. Her jerk of a husband had left her so unsure of herself sexually and of her judgment regarding men, that she had had to erect a shield around her heart in the form of an imaginary lover. In Rome, she had felt safe enough with him to reveal that she had no lover. And if God was good to him, he'd spend the rest of his life making her feel safe and secure. Starting with not having to tell her two weeks from now that he'd lost his business to his brother-in-law on a bet. If he could hold out fourteen more days, he'd take her in his arms and so worship her with his mouth, with his whole body, that she would never again doubt that she was beautiful, sexy and loved.

For now, all he could do was say, "Nonsense." Un-clenching the hands that ached to sculpt her body, he lifted her across his thigh and onto the floor beside him. Moving to sit before her, he caged her with his arms, then looked sternly into her eyes. "I could sit here and tell you you're as fine a specimen of womanhood as walks the earth, but it won't matter unless you believe it yourself. You've let Rance and Jillian poison you, Sarina. But there's an anti-dote and you've got to take it."

Sarina met his intense gaze, hearing advice that wasn't new but listening as if for the first time. There was no word for what she saw in Max's eyes but authority. Male authority. The kind that when genuine, like Max's, prods with one hand as it protects with the other. Even if those hands were at the end of satin sleeves, she liked it, a lot. "You're right, I know. I have to cry to cleanse my psyche. But for some reason, just now, telling you things I've never admitted to anyone—not even to myself—I don't feel like crying anymore." She clasped her hands around his muscled arm. "Maybe that's because I know I have a true friend who won't let me feel sorry for myself."

Max smiled, trying not to focus on her lips, so near and so soft, and so needing to be kissed. Needing his kiss. He decided he'd better give Father Nick's advice to keep moving one more try. "Of course, I don't have much personal experience with crying," he said, walking to the carved mantel and propping his elbow on it. "But I do know that if you want to see yourself differently, you have to behave differently. Sarina, before you can get back your self-confidence you have to face down your bogeypersons."

Her brows arrowing down, Sarina rose and joined Max at the fireplace, propping her elbow next to his. "Rance and Jillian?"

"Exactly. You have to show them that they didn't kill you, they made you stronger."

Sarina questioned him from the corner of her eye. "Nietzsche?"

"I thought I was quoting Oprah."

Laughing, they raised their propped forearms, their hands meeting in a variation of a high five. But their laughter faded as their fingers meshed, their palms joining like soul mates after years of wandering in search of each other.

"So, Boyfriend," Sarina said, stretching out her fingers, sliding her palm along his. "How do you suggest I get Rance and Jillian out of my system?"

Hearing her call him that name and imagining she'd meant it differently, Max felt an unbearable surge of heat from the palm of his hand to the core of his being, and elsewhere. Stepping away from her, he caught sight of her dining room. Shoving his hands in his pockets, he faced her. "Why not invite them to dinner?"

Sarina blurted out a single laugh. "Have those traitors

in my home? Serve them food at my table? I don't think so.'' She took their mugs to the kitchen.

Max followed her. ''Sarina, what better way to prove to yourself that you've moved on with your life than by proving it to the people who hurt you?''

After rinsing the mugs, she put them in the dishwasher, pondering. Had she moved on with her life? She'd certainly entered into a new and trusting friendship, one to celebrate. ''You may have a point.'' She shut the dishwasher with a solid thud. ''I'll do it. But on one condition. You have to be my guest along with the Dokters.''

''Oh, no. Leave me out of this,'' Max said. Raising his hands in protest, he walked through the hall, gathering his coat, wig and peignoir, then to the front door.

Sarina tracked him. ''But why not? Having them to dinner was your idea in the first place.''

''For one thing, Friends from Friends in High Places, aren't supposed to get personally involved with clients, and I've gone way over the line with you.'' He opened the door, then turned to her. ''I'm sorry, Sarina, but just by being here I've broken all the rules.''

She grabbed his arm, staying him. ''But you're part owner of the agency. You can suspend the rules for one night, can't you?''

''*No,* I can't. How would it look if the other Friends found out?'' *Or if Tony's detective found out?* Max was certain he was still the only one who knew he'd proved Tony's case, and with luck, he'd keep it that way. ''Besides, I'd only spoil the evening.''

Sarina batted her eyelids in mock astonishment. ''And how, pray tell?''

''Well, after what you told me tonight I'd have to punch out Rancid and Gilligan—''

''Jillian.'' She sucked in a smile.

Holding the doorknob, Max gazed down at her, his expression suddenly serious. How he ached to graze her cheek with his fingers. Instead, he leaned his head against the flat of the door. "I'm sure you see what I mean."

She did. He loved her. In his own way, Max loved her. She leaned her head against the door's edge. "Of course I do. You mean that you'll bring the wine."

"Right." With a smile, Max straightened. "Good night, Girlfriend."

Yawning, Sarina began to close the door behind him, then opened it again. "Max?"

He looked at her over his shoulder.

"I was just thinking, we spent the whole night talking about me. Now, you don't have to tell me if you don't want to, but I'd really like to know who hurt *my* best friend so I can punch him or her in the nose if *I* ever get the chance."

Max raised his arm, leaning on the jamb and drawing Sarina's gaze up to his. "She was my mother. No, she was my friend. And she never meant to hurt me." He looked away, then back. "She just died, Sarina. I was twelve and she died."

Sarina felt a stab beneath her left breast, an empathy that wounded her. She wanted to express it, but words were inadequate.

Max placed a kiss on the tips of his fingers then touched them to her lips, as if to assure her he understood what she would say if she could. "Get some rest," he said softly, then walked away.

Sarina locked her door, turned out the lights and slowly returned to her bedroom. She stood at the foot of her bed, knowing she was exhausted beyond endurance yet unable to lay her bones down. A new emotion was gathering force inside her, one so big she needed to make room for it. She needed to clear a place in her heart for the grief she felt for a twelve-year-old boy she'd never known, a boy who had long since grown into a man. One she dearly loved.

Throwing herself atop her comforter, she exploded with long overdue and soul-deep wails. They were untainted by anger at the people who—intentionally or not—had hurt her and Max, or by a sense that either of them had been victims, understandable as that might have been. Her sobs came from a place beyond pity for herself or even for Max, from an unexplored and much larger place inside her where she discovered her connection to the whole terrifyingly sad and awesomely enduring human race. For that, she had Max to thank.

When her tears receded at last, Sarina sat up, wiped her nose, then climbed off the bed and walked to her bathroom. She splashed cold water on her face, then grabbed a towel and dabbed the moisture away. She looked in the mirror, and seeing her red, swollen eyes, laughed out loud. She'd never looked worse nor felt stronger. She had finally cried her heart out. Better yet, a bigger heart had taken its place.

Who knew? she thought, looking toward her bedroom window and seeing ribbons of first light. *It might even be big enough to forgive Rance and Jillian.*

7

MINUTES AFTER SARINA had buzzed him into her building, Max tapped out an upbeat rhythm on her door. All in all, he was in high spirits tonight. He checked his watch: Friday, February 12th at 7:36 P.M. That meant he'd arrived in plenty of time to put his rare find, not one but two bottles of world-renowned Ken Wright Chardonnay on ice before the Dokters arrived. Even more important, it meant that in just two days, sixteen hours and twenty-four minutes, his bet with Tony would officially end.

Max had every hope of winning. The little round-faced P.I., who was probably in New Jersey by now after following him along the convoluted route he'd taken to Sarina's apartment, would have nothing incriminating to report, at least to this point. But time was now on Max's side.

That, and the fact that he wasn't the same man he'd been when he began his Friendship with Sarina. Although his desire for her was stronger than ever, he had made it his ally instead of his enemy. He'd even nurtured it, holding it in his heart as a commitment to her he looked forward to fulfilling. But first, he had to undo the harm that plastic-hearted plastic surgeon had done her. He had to win her trust, not just as a friend but as a man. And he knew exactly how. He'd sweep her off her feet, take her to undreamed-of heights of romance. He'd make her feel again like the delicious woman she was.

Only not before noon on Monday.

Hearing Max's knock, Sarina limped from her bedroom,

brandishing and cursing an expensive new shoe with a newly broken heel. Opening the door, she thrust the shoe in Max's face. "Do you see this?"

"It's not as though I could miss it," Max replied. He took the spikeless gold pump from Sarina, examined it, then examined her. Her hair, normally charmingly defiant, was now waging outright war with itself. Her makeup looked as though it had been applied during an earthquake. One strap of her gold dress flopped off her shoulder. "Let me guess, Rancid and Gilligan arrived early and one of them is now sporting the missing heel of this shoe in his or her head."

Sarina snatched the shoe back. "Don't be ridiculous!" Turning, she started for the kitchen.

"Whoa!" Kicking the door shut behind him, Max snagged her arm.

"What are you doing?"

Trying to keep my eyes off your beautiful bare back. "I just thought you might like your dress zipped."

"Zipper's stuck, of course." Turning her back to him and pinching in her waist, she sang a familiar tune. "That old Mann Whammy has me in its spell."

"Sarina, we've been over this," Max said, setting down the wine. "Your whammy is nothing more than a textbook example of self-fulfilling prophecy." Working her zipper, he erupted in a cold sweat at the sight of her hips undulating their assistance. "Do you mind?"

Sarina held still. "And I suppose you have an equally simple explanation of why my oven went on the blink today and wasn't fixed until twenty minutes ago?"

"Coincidence."

"Curse. This evening is too important to me for the Hex to resist sabotaging it." Zipped, Sarina hobbled to the kitchen.

Max followed those swaying hips, wine in hand, pulse rate in trouble. After putting the wine on the counter, he stepped to the sink, spritzed his face with cold water, and dabbed it with a paper towel. Thanking himself because he needed that, he turned to her. "Sarina, sabotage is in the eye of the beholder."

"No, it's in the hands of the florist."

Folding his arms, Max gave her a sidelong look. "Excuse me?"

Checking the progress of her specialty, Greek chicken, and finding none, she turned up the thermostat. Serving dried-out chicken, she figured, was better than having to come up with an extra half hour's worth of conversation with Benedict and Mrs. Arnold. She shut the oven door and threw the mitts on the counter. "Instead of the centerpiece I ordered, the florist delivered a red-and-white carnation heart with a banner that read 'Rest in Peace, BoBo'. If that isn't sabotage—"

"Actually, it sounds to me like one hell of a wake." Using the corkscrew she'd set out, Max opened the wine and filled two of the four crystal goblets on a tray. Handing one of them to Sarina, he raised his beneath a wry smile. "To BoBo."

Sarina laughed. "To BoBo."

As Max twined his arms with hers in a toast, he saw Sarina's broken shoe on the floor beside the kitchen table. Putting down his glass, he retrieved the shoe, snapping his fingers. "Nurse, severed heel. Bonding adhesive."

Sarina quickly produced both, then plunked down in a chair and watched him operate. If only he could cure what ailed her as easily. She had thought she could forgive Rance and Jillian. Now, she wasn't sure she could face them. "It's no use, Max," she said, taking another sip of wine. "I can't do it. I can't face Rance and Jillian after a year without—"

Max applied his strength, pushing the glued heel into the bottom of the shoe. "Without what?"

Sarina took another swallow. "Without a relationship."

Satisfied the heel was secure, he stooped and, cupping

her ankle, slipped the shoe onto her sweet foot. "You have a relationship. With me."

"I'm not talking about a platonic relationship, Max," she said, draining her glass.

Max felt a blow to his midsection and to his hope that she might, even now, feel a little something more for him than friendship. But if all he could ever be was her friend, he wouldn't shirk that. Slowly, he straightened and looked down at her. "Is the woman I saw bend hard-nosed businessmen to her will, now telling me she needs a man to face her ex-husband and ex-best friend?"

Sarina took a gulp of wine. "I know it's shallow of me, but you don't know Jillian. The woman is the all-time champion gloater." Walking to the counter, she refilled her glass, then propping her elbows on the black granite, focused on Max. "Friend, you've got to help me out here."

Max's brows gathered in puzzlement then lifted in horror. She was asking him to fake something he'd love to be, if only he could. "Oh no, Sarina," he said, his palms going up in protest. "I will not pretend to be your date."

As he stalked down the hall, Sarina followed him, glass in hand. "I don't want you to pretend to be my date."

"Good," he shot over his shoulder.

"I want you to pretend to be my fiancé."

Max came to a halt. Now she was asking him to rip his heart out. Slowly, he turned. "Why not your husband? I mean, if you really want to show them up, maybe I can run out and rent a baby."

Sarina leaned against the wall. "You don't have to be sarcastic. A simple engagement will do."

"No!"

"Why not?"

Caging her with his arms, Max took her left hand and wiggled it before her eyes. "For one thing, you don't have a ring."

"That's true," Sarina said, then pushed pursed lips to

one side. "I know! I can tell them the diamond is so large I have to keep it in a bank vault."

Letting go of her hand with a chiding look, Max walked to the bar in the living room and removed an ice bucket.

Taking another sip of wine, Sarina stood behind him. "All right, so you're not crazy about that idea. How about I tell them we had to take it back to the jeweler for sizing?"

"How about you tell them we're just friends?"

"But, Max, you're so incredibly attractive that if I said we're just friends, you know what they'd think, don't you?"

Max barely heard the question. He was still hearing her say he was incredibly attractive, and his hopes rose again. "No, what?"

Sarina began turning a circle, her free hand gesturing. "Well, they'd think there was something the matter with me. 'Poor Sarina,' they'd say. 'She must have bedroom problems.'" She took his hand. "The one thing I won't be able to bear is their pity, Max. That's why you have to be my fiancé."

Putting down the bucket, Max folded his arms. "Now, I get it. You want me to act like I can't keep my hands off you, like you drive me insane with desire. Well, you—" He breathed out, then swallowed hard. He'd almost said it. Lord help him, he'd almost told her that she did. "You don't know what you're asking."

"Yes, I do, Max." Sarina lifted his hand to her cheek in entreaty. "You don't have to make a big show of it. You don't even have to kiss me. Just take my hand once in a while. And put your arm around me, like you did the other night, in front of the fire."

Gazing down at her, Max melted, as if he were seeing one of those sponsor-a-waif pleas on TV. To date, he had six waifs from Mississippi to the Philippines. Still—

"That's the buzzer. Oh, Max—" Sarina drained her second glass. "They're here!"

"I'll get the door," he said, taking the glass, then pointing her toward her bedroom. "You'd better do something with your hair and makeup."

Scurrying toward her bedroom, Sarina paused. "Please, Max. I'll never ask another favor of you. I promise."

"Sarina, I can't—" She'd gone before he could finish refusing her request. Muttering, he stomped to the door and buzzed the Dokters into the building. As he waited for them to arrive, he paced. "I can't do this," he spluttered. "I'm no good at pretending, especially when I'm not pretending." He might forget he was pretending and kiss her. *One kiss and I'm a dead man. I'm a—*

"Fiancé," he said, answering the knock at the door and extending his hand toward the couple gaping at him. "You must be Jillian and Rance. I'm Max, Sarina's fiancé."

SAVORING ONE OF SARINA'S feta-stuffed mushroom appetizers and thoroughly beguiled, Max observed her sudden transformation from waif to serene and gracious hostess. He wondered which was more responsible—the wine or his announcement of their engagement to Rance and Jillian. But watching her field the Dokters' persistent questions about their wedding plans with answers so ingeniously vague they sounded mysteriously romantic, he realized she was simply a consummate actress.

"Where do you think you might honeymoon?" Jillian pressed, as Sarina ushered her guests to the table.

"Well, Max and I did just spend three glorious days at the most romantic hotel on the Via Veneto," she replied, gazing at Max.

The light in her eyes, he thought, put the candles on her table to shame. If only it was evidence of real romantic feelings for him instead of her considerable theatrical talents.

"I think that would be an ideal setting for a honeymoon, don't you, darling?" she asked him.

Max cleared his throat, his imagination running wild. "Incredible," he said, picturing them making love in that little walled garden she had found so enchanting. Suddenly, the room seemed unbearably hot.

Sarina felt her skin flush. She'd probably had too much wine. And definitely, too much Max. She had to remind herself that he couldn't possibly be looking at her the way she imagined he was, like a man in love with a woman he was eager to make his wife. That he couldn't possibly be envisioning the paradise she was picturing—the two of them, making love in her secret garden in Rome. If ever she needed a reality check, it was now.

"I'd like to propose a toast," reality said, and not a second too soon. Standing beside his wife, Rance raised his glass. "To Max and Sarina. May you always be as happy as Pumpkin and I have been this last year."

"Not so fast." With a sly look, Jillian clicked her nails on the side of her glass. "I'm not convinced you two really are engaged."

Sarina swallowed hard. This much reality she didn't need. "Why would we say we were if we weren't?"

"I can't imagine," Jillian replied, a laugh lifting one corner of her mouth. "All I know is that you two haven't kissed once all evening."

Max and Sarina snapped panicked looks at each other, then trailed their eyes to each other's lips as though they'd never seen lips before.

Sarina knew she had to stop this ridiculous charade before it went any further. *Because I love him.* Because kissing her would be painful for him and she wouldn't hurt him for the world.

"It's unfortunate that some people think sex is a measure of love," she said, arching a brow as she turned to Jillian. "What Max and I feel for each other is immeasurable."

"It's not only immeasurable, it's invisible," Jillian replied.

Sarina gulped air. "Jillian—"

"Angel," Max said, taking Sarina in his arms. Looking at her plump, glistening mouth, he couldn't believe that he was about to claim it at last, but not for himself. For her pride. "What's there to hide?"

Sarina returned the mischievous glint in Max's eyes. She would have loved to give him a poke in the ribs, but at the moment, it took all she had to breathe. She could hardly believe he was holding her so close. He should have been an actor. "Nothing, darling," she replied through clenched teeth.

Crushing her to him, Max turned Sarina away from the Dokters' prying, skeptical eyes. Touching the tips of his fingers to her cheek, he slowly brought his lips nearer to hers.

Sarina felt a tingle, as though lightning were about to strike. Her, at any rate. "You don't have to do this," she whispered, hardly hearing herself over the pounding in her ears.

"Jillian will never let you live it down if I don't," he whispered back.

Sarina gazed up at him, resisting the temptation to search for her Eden in his eyes. "I won't look at you," she murmured. "That will make it easier for both of us."

I doubt that, Max thought. Nevertheless, he followed her example, closing his own eyes and holding out hope that the briefest of kisses would quench the burning on his lips, the conflagration in his soul. Bending over her, he put his lips on hers, lightly, only to be overpowered by a backdraft of desire. A flame of passion torched his desire, long denied and quickly ignited, and he opened his mouth.

As Max's tongue scorched the recesses of her mouth, Sarina clasped her arms around his neck. She felt him lift her off the floor, like some hungry blaze needing to consume her body and soul. As he tightened his arms around her and deepened his kiss, Sarina became one with the blaze she was fueling.

With her fingers twining in the hair at the nape of his neck, her tongue like licks of flame reaching to his core, Max knew he was dangerously close to combustion. Perhaps he'd already gone up in smoke, he thought, hearing a siren.

It was only Rance, providing sound effects. "Perhaps we should forget the wine, Pumpkin," he said to Jillian, "and douse these two with a pitcher of ice water."

Max and Sarina opened their eyes, each seeing embers in the other's gaze. Each telling themselves they were only seeing what they wanted to see.

"I think we all need to cool off," Jillian said, fanning herself. Then, "What a marvelous idea I've just had!"

Max had some fairly marvelous ideas of his own, beginning with telling Rance and Jillian to start the salad course without them then, whisking Sarina to the bedroom. Where she would remind him they were just friends. Without taking his gaze from hers, he relinquished her, sliding her body along his to the floor.

Sarina heard a vague mention of cooling off. She needed to, desperately. "What idea?" she murmured, still gazing at Max.

Jillian explained that her boss had rented a two-bedroom chalet in the Catskills for the weekend, but discovering he wouldn't be able to use it, offered it to her and Rance. "So I was thinking, wouldn't it be a wonderful way to celebrate two momentous events?"

Reflecting the puzzlement in one another's eyes, Max and Sarina turned to Jillian. "What two events?" Sarina asked.

Rance put his arm around his wife. "What Pumpkin is proposing, Sarina—and I must say with her typical big-heartedness—is that we three celebrate our reconciliation, along with your engagement to Max, of course."

Thinking that Jillian's heart indeed knew no bounds, especially when it came to her best friend's husband, she said, "I still don't understand."

"I do," Max said, squeezing Sarina's hand as sheer terror coursed through his veins. "I think they want us to go to the Catskills with them."

"Exactly," Jillian cried. "Won't that be fun?"

Sarina stood benumbed, her mouthing hanging open. "But—" But she and Max would have to sleep in the same room, in the same bed.

"Unless, of course, you still have hard feelings toward Rance and me," Jillian added.

"Well, no. I mean…" Sarina looked helplessly at Max.

Max had now had about enough of Pumpkin and her plastic prince. They'd almost totally destroyed Sarina's faith in her fellow man and now they wanted even greater assurance than this dinner should have given them that they were forgiven. "Frankly, Jillian, I wouldn't blame Sarina if she did hold a grudge," he said of the woman who had helped him to resolve his own anger. Looking at Sarina, he smiled proudly. "But my girl is a better person than that."

Hearing him call her not Girlfriend, but his girl, Sarina's vision swam.

Thinking she looked woozy, probably from too much wine rather than passion, Max spanned his hands around her waist and drew her close.

"She has no reason to hold a grudge," Rance put in. "Now that she has you."

Pressing her hands to Max's solid chest, Sarina gaped at Rance. She could hardly contain her indignation at hearing him imply that her engagement to Max meant he could finally get her off his conscience. But he wouldn't get off so easily, because she wouldn't allow him to make Max out to be just some guy she was using to forget an unfaithful husband. Because Max wasn't just some guy. "That's right," she said, stiffening her spine as she wrapped her arms around Max's waist. "I have a real man now."

Gazing at her with wonderment, Max stood taller.

Jillian put her hand on her hip. "So, don't real men spend the weekend in the Catskills?"

"Pumpkin!"

Jillian patted her husband's cheek. "I'm just trying to find out if Max and Sarina are coming with us." She looked at the two of them. "Well, are you?"

Meeting the challenge to their own and each other's dignities, Max and Sarina turned on Jillian like a two-pronged fork. "Yes!"

"Here's to friendship, then," Rance said, lifting his glass.

Raising their own glasses, Max and Sarina, their indignation suddenly spent, cast fatalistic looks at one another. "Yeah," they mumbled. "To friendship."

"MAX?" Father Nick DeGrasso spoke through a yawn. "What am I saying? Of course, it's you. Everybody else I know restricts their spiritual crises to business hours."

"I'm sorry, Nick. I know it isn't even light yet," Max said, tossing a pair of heavy socks into a canvas bag. "But I'll be leaving here soon and I couldn't go without talking to you."

"About the woman you don't know what to do about, right?"

"Right." Max let out a breath. "I'm going to be sleeping with her."

There was a long pause, then, "Confessions are every Saturday from three to five. In the *afternoon*."

"No, I didn't mean it like that," Max said, raking back his hair. He plunked down on the bed. "Look, it's a long, complicated story that I don't have time to go into right now. But the bottom line is that we're taking a weekend ski trip and we're going to be sharing a bedroom. Of course, she thinks I think of her only as a friend—"

"Does she frequently share bedrooms with her male friends?"

"She doesn't have any other male friends. In fact, there aren't any other men in her life, period."

"How do you know that?"

"She told me." Max heard the priest clear his throat.

"Max, my son, are you sure you know women as well as you think you do?"

Max massaged the throbbing pain above his eyes. "I know *this* woman, Nick, and I'd trust her with my life. And as far as the weekend trip goes, you can take my word for it—it's all perfectly innocent."

"Then, why are you calling me?"

Max shot off the bed. "Because I want to keep it that way! At least until noon on Monday." He rubbed the back of his neck. "What should I do, Nick?"

"I don't see that you have any choice," Father Nick said, sounding rather stern. "This woman views you as nothing more than a friend and that's exactly how you'll have to conduct yourself."

Pulling open a drawer, Max removed a turtleneck and a sweater. "That's just it. After last night, I think she might feel something more than friendship toward me."

"Last night?"

"It was all supposed to be an act," he said, stuffing the items in the bag. "I mean, we even joked about what terrific performances we gave. Still, I can't stop thinking about the way she held on to me when I kissed her—"

"You kissed her?"

"Yeah."

"On the mouth?"

Max sighed. "Oh, yeah." He heard the priest's bed creak.

"Max, exactly what is your definition of 'perfectly innocent'?"

Max straddled the chair beside his bed. "Nick, Father, please. Just tell me what to do. I can't lie beside this woman and not tell her how I feel about her, and if I tell her how I feel about her and she gets offended and maybe complains to Tony—"

"How *do* you feel about her, Max?"

Suddenly, Max realized he had never said the words out loud, not about any woman let alone *to* any woman. And now he was about to tell, of all people, a priest. "I love her, Father. With all my heart and soul."

"As a friend?"

"Yes, as a friend. My best friend. And more."

"Yet, you've never more than kissed her, and then, just once?"

"Just once. But I knew before then that I wanted to spend the rest of my life with her." A long pause followed Max's reply.

"Max, would you like me to tell you now how many angels can fit on the head of a pin?"

Holding the phone away from his ear, Max looked at it, wondering if he'd heard correctly. But after all, he had awakened the priest. He owed him a little humoring. "Sure."

Father Nick's voice delivered a smile. "Not as many as are in your heart."

Max smiled back. "Thanks, Father. Maybe *they* can tell me what to do tonight."

AFTER LOCKING THE DOOR to her apartment, Sarina stooped to pick up her suitcase. Although she'd packed lightly, it tested her strength.

Just as the next thirty-six hours were about to do. She didn't know how she was going to get through them without telling Max how she really felt about him. Deceiving

Rance and Jillian was one thing, but withholding the truth from her best friend was no longer an option. Not after the way he'd pretended to kiss her last night.

In spite of the way they'd congratulated themselves on their sterling performances, that kiss had crossed the threshold of her tolerance. From now on, she wasn't going to be able to pretend away the quivering that started whenever Max came near her, let alone when they would share a bed. She was going to have to tell him.

Trudging to the elevator, she stopped at Jack's door and knocked. She heard his puppy yap, then the chain slide from its track.

"Sarina?" Jack, holding the little black dog, looked her up and down, squinting. "And where are we off to this time? London? Paris? Stockholm?"

"The Catskills."

"How depressing."

"You're telling me." Sarina repositioned the purse strap that had fallen from her shoulder. "You'll keep an eye out for any signs of smoke, burst pipes—"

"Famine and pestilence? But of course."

Thanking him, Sarina turned to leave, then paused. "Jack?"

"Si?"

"Would it bother you very much to sleep with me?"

Jack's eyes fully opened for the first time that morning. "Hearing our biological clock tick, are we?"

Sarina looked at him askance. "Huh?"

He turned a palm up. "You are looking for a sperm donor, aren't you?"

Sarina smiled. "No, that's not what I meant. But thanks for volunteering." She leaned in the doorway. "What I'm wondering is, if you and I found ourselves having to share a bed, just how uncomfortable would you feel?"

Jack folded his arms. "That depends. Could I bring a Ouija board and some really scary movies?"

Sarina chuckled. "In other words, we could have a pajama party."

"I'd even bring the chips and dip."

Turning, Sarina leaned her back against the outside wall and faced the elevator. "But what if you knew I was in love with you?"

Stepping outside his door, Jack stood before Sarina. "I think that would be very embarrassing for you and your friend, darling," he said soberly. "It might be better to pretend otherwise until—"

"Until what?"

Jack shrugged. "Until you're not in love with him anymore."

Smiling sadly, Sarina pushed off the wall. "Thanks, Jack, but I don't think I can wait forever."

As Rance brought his Mercedes to a stop outside the chalet overlooking a mountain glistening with snow, Jillian leaned against the front passenger door, clutching her side. "Oh, Max, stop. If I laugh any harder I won't be able to stand it." She looked at Sarina, sitting slumped in the corner of the back seat, next to Max. "No wonder you're so crazy about this man. He must have you howling from morning to night."

Sarina slid a glance at Max. During the nearly two-hour drive to the ski resort, he'd been a one-man comedy caravan, yukking it up with Rance and Jillian until she thought she would scream. He was her best friend. Couldn't he tell her heart was breaking? "Yeah. Sometimes he even makes me cry," she murmured.

Rance turned to the back seat, dangling two sets of keys and faintly resembling a used-car salesman. "Is everybody ready to have a good time?"

Sarina looked out her window at a chair lift in the distance. "I'm ready to hit the slopes," she said. *At least they're not the skids, not yet.* She'd hit those later, after she told Max that she was deeply and hopelessly in love with him and he responded with a kiss—goodbye.

Max rubbed his hands together. "Me, too," he said, entirely too cheerily for Sarina's liking.

"To tell you the truth," Rance said, with a wink at his wife, "Pumpkin and I didn't exactly come here for the skiing."

Jillian grabbed one of the sets of keys from him. "But we know you two won't mind being on your own." Grinning, she tossed the keys at Sarina.

Scooping them in cupped hands, Sarina knew they would open more than just the door to the chalet. They would open the final chapter of her relationship with Max. As Rance and Jillian got out of the car, Sarina removed one of the two keys from the ring and held it out to Max. "Sir, your freedom."

Max looked at the key, knowing it represented, as Sarina had just said, what he'd always wanted from a woman. The freedom to come and go as he pleased, no strings attached. What supreme irony, he thought, that the one woman who was demanding no commitment from him was the only woman he'd ever wanted to be completely committed to. *Forget irony,* he thought, taking the key. He was paying, at last, for his sins.

THAT NIGHT, Max started back from the mountain after ten. Hours earlier, when Sarina had said she'd had enough skiing for one day, he'd told her he was just hitting his stride and wanted to make a few more runs. The truth was, he was cold and every muscle in his body ached. He'd have given anything to go back to the chalet, sip a brandy with her in front of the fire, then get into bed. It was the thought of that last item that kept him going up and down that damn mountain until, realizing he was so tired he'd nearly slammed into a tree, he decided to face the music. Face Sarina.

But first, he had to face himself. When he and Sarina had shared a hot chocolate in the lodge at the base of the mountain, he'd realized he no longer cared whether he won or lost his bet. In fact, he deserved to lose it. He'd sworn he could remain personally uninvolved with the client Tony had assigned him. But he was more than involved, he was in love, and with a woman who had told her former husband that at last, she'd found a real man. A real man wouldn't claim the spoils of a wager he hadn't really won.

Besides, he wouldn't be the only person who knew the truth. One day, Sarina would find out about the bet, and if he'd claimed to have won it, she would know he'd lied, cheated. He'd lose her respect and that was a hell of a lot worse than losing the business.

Still, doing the right thing wasn't going to be easy, he thought as he entered the resort's office. But if his darling Sarina could face the people who'd torn up her life, he could face the music.

He asked the desk clerk for stationery, then took the sheets she gave him to a nearby desk. When he'd finished the letter Tony would find on his fax machine at the office Monday morning, he returned to the main desk.

"Would you like me to fax that for you now?" the clerk asked.

Max paused, asking himself one last time if he was really ready to exchange a thriving business for the truth, for his self-respect. Finally, he broke into a broad grin. "I'd like nothing better," he said, handing her the pages.

Something else a real man didn't do was sleep with the woman he loved without telling her how he felt and finding out her feelings for him. Nor did he sleep with a woman without protecting her.

He asked the clerk for directions to the nearest open drugstore.

IN THE CHALET, Sarina sat in front of the massive stone fireplace, hugging her knees, and trying not hear the noises coming from the Dokters' bedroom. At least three of the four of us are having a good time, she thought. She'd left Max on the slopes hours ago, never having seen a man so intent on getting the most out of his lift ticket. If he didn't return soon, she'd have to go to bed without him. Without telling him her true feelings about their kiss last night.

Hearing what sounded a lot like a headboard banging against the wall, Sarina got up and walked to the vast window overlooking the mountain. Seeing the lit trails, she wondered if Max was still out there somewhere, testing the limits of his endurance. And hers. Maybe she ought to take Jack's advice, forget about making a clean breast of her feelings for Max, and go to sleep.

Did I hear something about baring our breasts again?

"Be quiet," Sarina muttered, addressing her inner nag. "I was merely debating whether or not to tell Max that I'm in love with him. And I've decided against it."

But honesty is the best—

"Not this time," she said, turning from the window. "My mind's made up, and you know that once I do that—"

"Girlfriend?" Max stood in the open doorway, gazing about the room. "You talking to yourself?"

Sarina watched him close the door, then advance toward her, shedding his ski jacket. His underlying frame was muscular yet elegant in a turtleneck and tight ski pants. His hair appeared darker than it really was, cast in shadow as the light from the fire in the hearth bathed his features. Especially his eyes, so bright, as though they'd just seen an angel. God, he was so beautiful.

At that moment, she knew she'd been right to decide not to confess her love. She wanted to remember him the way he looked now, so warm and vital and whole. Not the way he would look after she'd made him feel the way she had no right to make him feel, that he'd let her down. "Rance and Jillian don't seem to be in a very talkative mood," she said with a laugh and a nod toward the Dokters' bedroom.

Lowering his head, Max stared at her from beneath raised brows. "Just think, that could be you in there."

Sarina stared back at him, and when she couldn't stand it any longer, she exploded with rolicking laughter that sent her to her knees, and finally, onto her back in front of the hearth. Max sat facing the fire. He lifted her head, cradling it in his lap, stroking her hair. "I take it that means you're finally over the Plastic Pumpkin Affair?"

Sarina looked at him upside down. "The wh—? Oh." At last getting Max's reference to Rance's profession and his nauseating nickname for Jillian, she started laughing all over again. Finally regaining sobriety, she said, "You know, Max, I'm glad we came up here with them. They really are very much in love and I can't blame them for that. Whatever I felt they did to me, I've let it go." Sitting up, she turned to him. "You helped me to do that."

"Did I?" Max traced the outlines of her fingers, pressed to the floor. "How?"

Sarina watched his finger tracing hers. "Remember the night you told me about your mother's death?"

Surprised, Max looked up. "Yes."

Sarina peered at the fire. "After you left, I cried so hard I felt I'd turned myself inside out. But it was a good cry, Max, because you made me feel things again, not just for myself but for others." She gazed at him. "That's what your friendship has done for me. Brought me back into the human race."

Gazing into her eyes, like blue topaz in the red-gold setting of her hair, Max thought, for a brief moment, he really was seeing an angel. Then he thought that, just maybe, he was getting a sign from one of the angels Nick had said was in his heart. A sign that now was the time to speak his heart. "Sarina, if you say I helped you, I'm glad. But all I can think of is what—"

"Yes, Max?"

Not so fast, he cautioned himself. Remember what you vowed to do to make her love you the way you love her? You promised to sweep the romantic heights with her feet. No, that can't be it. Sweep her feet off heights of romance? Close enough. "Sarina, all I can think of is what our friendship has meant to me." *Keep that up and she'll be swooning in no time, from boredom,* Max thought, lowering his head to his hand.

"Me, too," Sarina replied, patting his hand. "On that note," she added, faking a yawn, "I think I'll turn in." She could at least pretend to be asleep before he came to bed.

Max took her hands in his. "I was hoping we could stay up a while and talk."

"Couldn't we talk in the morning, Max?" Talk was the last thing Sarina wanted to do, considering the only six words she could think to say at the moment were "I'm in love with you, Max." Getting to her feet, she looked down at him. "I'm really done in."

And I'm done for, Max thought. He knew he couldn't go into that bedroom with her, lie silently down beside her in the dark cocoon of her intoxicating scent and not resort to eating his pillow. "Look, Girlfriend," he said, standing. "Why don't I sleep right here on the couch? You can bet that marital marathon in there won't be over before morning, so they'll never know we slept apart."

"S'fine with me," Sarina said, shrugging and never letting on that she'd breathed a sigh of relief. "Well, good night."

"Good night."

"Hello!"

Max and Sarina did about-faces, their gazes falling wide-eyed on the Dokters emerging, at last, from their love nest.

"You two still up?" Jillian asked, then without waiting

for an answer, added, "We thought you'd have gone to bed long ago."

Staring at each other, Max and Sarina stammered a duet.

"Well—"

"We were just—"

"Don't stay up on our account," Rance said, tightening his robe as he padded toward the kitchen. "Pumpkin and I are going to grab some of that leftover pizza we had delivered, and then you won't see us again until morning."

Jillian followed Rance, flicking on the light as he removed the pizza box from the counter and brought it to the table.

"You two go on to bed," Jillian said, taking a seat. "Rance and I will see that the fire's out."

Swallowing the lump in her throat, Sarina said goodnight to the Dokters and walked into the bedroom. Max gathered his jacket and followed her. Shutting the door, he hung the jacket on the back of it, then joined Sarina at the foot of the bed. They stood side by side in the semidark, looking down at it.

"It's only a double," Sarina said.

"Yeah, small." Max looked at her. "Which side do you want?"

"The right side," Sarina replied. "If I can find it."

8

IN SEMIDARKNESS, Max and Sarina stood on opposite sides of the bed, their backs to each other as they undressed.

Hearing the unzipping of her jeans, Max froze at the image of them slowly sliding down her oscillating hips. When static electricity crackled as she lifted her sweater over her head, he pictured her beautiful back, naked to the waist. Still visualizing, he saw her slowly turn toward him, her smile slight and her eyes luminous with desire. Then, she climbed on the bed, took his hand and placed it on her breast. He shivered.

Hearing the whoosh of cotton as he drew his undershirt up his torso, Sarina froze, clutching the jeans she'd just removed. She pictured the unveiling of a classic sculpture of a male nude, prompting awe and inviting touch. She raised her hand as if to run her fingers over the hard, rippled surface of his chest, the straining sinews in his arms, the—

"Uh, excuse me."

"I'm so sorry!" With a start, Sarina brought one hand to her mouth. The other held her jeans over her breasts.

"You didn't do anything. I just want to get my pajama bottoms." Max pointed past her to his bag on a chair in the corner.

"Oh. No problem." *Yes, problem*, Sarina thought as he squeezed through the narrow space between her and the dresser, making all her flesh a panic of want and need. Her gaze followed a treacherous shaft of moonlight on his naked back as he headed to the corner, where he bent over his suitcase. As he rummaged through it, her eyes traced the routes of muscles mapping his back and shoulders. When he turned, they sped across his chest's hard, glistening terrain, then down narrow straits to his waist. As he came toward her and she felt her heart pound, pistonlike, she was unaware that she was lowering her hands.

"Excuse me, again," he said, pausing before her, searching her gaze in the shadows.

"No—" Sarina cleared her throat "—problem."

Maybe not for you, Max thought as he stood before her, his eyes limning the outline of her slender throat and bare shoulders, caressing the soft mounds capped with the lacy, white bra that glowed opalescent in the moonlight. He cleared his throat and spoke over his fast-beating heart. "Can I get you anything? A cup of coffee, maybe?"

Sarina blinked. "Max, why would I want coffee just as I'm about to go to sleep?"

So you'll be awake when I tell you I love you. "Brandy, then." *So you'll warm to my proposal of marriage.*

"Max, I just want to lay my head on the pillow and go to sleep." *And be dead, for a few blessed hours, to my impossible love for you.*

Max lifted his fingers to her face, but fearing that the slightest touch could unleash a torrent of premature declarations of his love, he lowered them. "Good night again, then."

When she'd felt his touch near her cheek, Sarina held her breath. Now, she released it. "Yeah, g'night."

Willing his feet to move, Max rounded to his side of the bed. As he stood with his back to Sarina, pulling off his ski pants, he lost his balance. Hopping a circle, he saw that she stood facing the corner, her arms in the air as she started to put on a long, soft gown. Moonlight silhouetted the side of one small, bare, beautifully shaped breast. He stood for a moment, adoring her, barely enduring his aching need for her, until he'd found himself with only one choice.

Quickly turning away, he scrambled into his pajama bottoms and slipped quickly beneath the covers. He pulled them up to his chin and held them there, and rocked on the waves of his own heavy breathing.

Lifting the blankets, Sarina got into bed. She folded the sheet over the covers, pulled them up to her ears, then assumed a funereal position—legs stretched stiff, hands folded atop her abdomen, eyes wide open. She let out a long sigh.

Max did the same, lowering his arm to his side and unintentionally grazing Sarina's hip. His hand shot outside the blankets. "Sorry!"

Sarina felt an agony of thwarted desire shoot from her hip to the top of her head, bringing hot, bitter tears with it. She squeezed her eyes shut. "No...problem," she murmured and turned on her side. But the tears wouldn't retreat. As they gathered in strength and numbers, her fight to contain them grew so desperate that her whole body shook with the effort.

"Sarina?" Max turned toward her, cupping her shoulder. "Are you crying?"

"No!" Sniffing, she drew three shallow rasping breaths.

"Yes, you are!" Reaching across to her other shoulder, he turned her toward him. "Angel, what is it? What's wrong? You can tell me."

"No, I ca-a-a-n't." She held her hands to her mouth.

Gently, Max took her hands in his. "Yes, you can. I'm your best friend, remember?"

She wailed louder.

"I'm not your best friend?"

"Yes, you are. But—" What was the use of hiding her feelings any longer? He knew her so well that sooner or later, he'd detect that she was keeping a secret from him. "Oh, Ma-a-a-ax. You don't *luh-uh-uhve* me!"

Max held her tight. "Shhh, Girlfriend. You know I do."

She pounded a weak fist on his chest. "I don't mean just as a…a…a friend."

Max's breath caught, his eyes widened. "You don't?"

She shook her head, rubbing her forehead against his chest. "No-o-o."

"Oh." Max felt her head rise and fall with his chest—and the hope burgeoning inside him. Dry-mouthed, he said, "Neither do I."

Instantly, Sarina's tears turned off. Her brows puckered. "You don't?"

"No. That's what I wanted to talk to you about." Taking her by the shoulders, he pierced through the darkness with his gaze, finding hers. "I want you to listen to what I have to say, Sarina. Don't interrupt."

She couldn't have if she'd wanted to. She was wide-eyed and speechless as Max wrapped her again in his arms, pressing her cheek to the wall of his chest, and stroked his thumb across her lips.

"Sarina," he began, tilting his head atop hers, "a little while ago, you told me what you believed I'd done for you. Well, do you know what you've done for me?"

She started to lift her head but he pressed it back down.

"You allowed me to redeem myself," he said, his palm coursing her arm, the heel of his hand lightly brushing the side of her breast. "By placing your complete trust in me, you gave me the chance to prove that I didn't have to fear letting a woman down the way I must have always felt I'd let my mother down. Do you realize what a breakthrough that was for me? You completely changed the way I relate to women."

Sarina gulped. "Completely?"

After reaching to his right and, switching on the lamp beside the bed, Max took her face in his hands. "Completely," he said. "You made me a new man. Sarina, I love you so much and I can't wait to show you. I want to worship you with my whole body.'' He lowered his mouth to hers.

Sarina pushed his chest. "Your whole body? Wouldn't you like to start with maybe a wink?'' She blinked her left eye at him. "Or a handshake!''

Taking the hand she held out to him, Max drew her back into his embrace, laughing. "Sarina, you don't understand. I have years of living like half a man to make up for and I want to do it all with you. Only you.''

When he lifted her chin, obviously intent on kissing her, she reached up and squished his face between her hands. "It's my turn now, Max. And don't interrupt.''

"Uh oh I uh an,'' he mumbled through her grip.

"What?''

"I don't think I can,'' he repeated, prying her hands away and holding them. "Look, Sarina, darling—''

"No!''

The vehemence of her resistance so stunned Max that he dropped her hands. Watching her back away from him to the opposite corner of the bed, he reminded himself that he still needed to go slow with her, woo her, until she believed he'd never betray her. Holding up his hand, he sat back against the headboard. "It's okay. I'm listening now.''

Pressing her fingertips to her forehead, she tried to think, for both of them. "Max,'' she began, putting her praying hands to her lips. "Don't you think you ought to slow down a bit, take things one step at a time? I mean, how do you know that what you feel for me isn't just gratitude?''

He rolled his eyes, then smiled at her. "Sarina, I said you'd changed me, not hatched me.'' Resolving not to reach for her but unable to remain still, he shot forward on his hands and knees.

Thinking he was going to make a grab for her, Sarina fell back. Her head dangled over the edge of the bed. The next thing she saw was Max peering down at her. Circling his arm around her waist, he smiled.

"Don't you think I know the difference between grati-
ude and true, romantic love?"

"If you say so," she said, not wanting to agitate him
further. "Max?"

"Yes, Angel?"

"The blood is rushing to my head." After he helped her
up, apologizing, she said, "The point is, Max, that a change
his sudden and drastic... I'm not sure it's such a good
thing."

Feeling a stab of dread, Max sat on a haunch. "Sarina,
did I misunderstand you? Don't you want us to be more
than friends?"

She laid her hand atop his. "Oh God, Max, I do. I'm so
in love with you sometimes I think I'll die if I can't have
you."

Grinning wildly, he cupped her cheek. "Then what's the
problem?"

Sarina shivered at his touch, loving it and at the same
time not knowing whether she should, just yet. "I just want
you to be sure."

He pulled her to him, bringing them nose-to-nose. "I've
never been surer of anything in my life."

*This is too fast, too sudden, too potentially heartbreaking
for both of us,* Sarina thought as her eyes crossed on the
bridge of his nose. "Look, Max, will you do something for
me?"

"What do you want? The moon? I'll lasso it for you."

"I know, Jimmy Stewart, *It's a Wonderful Life,* 1946,"
Sarina said. "But Max, this is no time for movie trivia."

"Sorry," he replied, scrunching her shoulders. "But you
make me so crazy for you I don't know what I'm saying
half the time. Seriously, whatever you want, just name it."

"Coffee."

Max released her. "What?"

"I'd like that coffee now," Sarina said.

His shoulders slumping, Max sighed. Sweeping Sarina

off her feet was proving a little more complicated than he'd thought it would be. But whatever it took, he was the man to do it. Shoving off the bed, he looked at her from the door. "Is instant okay?"

She shook her head. "Brewed."

"As you wish," he said and left.

"Cary Elwes, *Princess Bride,* 1987," Sarina muttered as she scurried off the bed and shut the door. Max's ski jacket fell off the hook, and tossing it on the bed, she scrambled to the nightstand. There, she ferreted her planner from her purse, found the phone number she needed, and dialed. After three rings, a surprisingly alert female voice answered.

"Dr. Barrett Brown? This is Sarina Mann." She cupped the mouthpiece. "Listen, I don't have much time. He wants to make love to me."

"Who wants to make love to you?"

Sarina cast a wary eye at the door. "Max!"

"Who's Max?"

Sarina rolled her eyes. The therapist ought to refund her money for not listening. "You *know,* my Friend."

"Max? Not Max Evangelist!"

Sarina froze. In her panic, she'd forgotten she'd previously disguised his identity.

"Sarina? I thought you said his name was Mr. Stan and that he was gay."

Whether or not Dr. Barrett Brown knew Max was gay didn't matter now. The important thing was his mental and emotional health. "I do mean Max and he *is* gay. And he claims I've changed him."

"The only thing you appear to have changed, Sarina—" The therapist giggled, then sounding as if she'd turned away from the phone, whispered, "Henley, you naughty boy!"

Sarina gathered she'd called at a bad time. Or maybe it was a good time. "Doctor?"

"As I was saying the only thing you appear to have

changed is his strategy. If Max Evangelist is gay, I'm Our Lady of Lourdes."

Sarina shot to her full height. "But, what about…" She described the conversation she'd overheard with someone named Mike, then the encounter Max had had with Mike Preston.

The doctor tsked. "Mike Preston is a nutcase who wrongly blames Max for breaking up his marriage. I know because Max asked me to talk to him to try to find out if he was potentially dangerous. And as for that phone conversation, I wouldn't be surprised if you overheard Max talking to his sister Micah, Mike for short. She's expecting her first baby."

Dumbstruck, Sarina sat on the bed. "Are you absolutely sure Max isn't even a little gay?"

"Sarina, trust me." Julia Barrett Brown lowered her voice to an almost inaudible hush. "For a short time, I dated the man."

In a daze, Sarina hung up. Soon, though, her mind reeled with questions. If Max wasn't gay, why had he practically withdrawn from her in horror during the early stages of their relationship? Why had he come to her apartment that night in drag? Maybe he'd realized she thought he was gay and decided to play along with her. But why? What could he possibly have to gain by posing as a homosexual? she asked herself as she leaned on Max's ski jacket. Especially now that he'd claimed to be in love with her, having pretended to be gay made no sense at all.

Idly playing with the zipper on a pocket in Max's jacket, she thought of what Dr. Barrett Brown had just said. The only thing she had probably changed about Max was his strategy. What strategy? Sitting up, deep in thought and absently staring at Max's jacket, Sarina saw a slender package in the pocket she'd unzipped. As she removed it, her eyes grew enormous.

"Ugh!" She pounded her forehead with the heel of her hand. "And I congratulated him on how good he'd been at faking that kiss!'' Suddenly, Sarina knew exactly what Max had been scheming for since the day he walked into her office.

STANDING OUTSIDE the closed bedroom door, Max balanced a tray holding a steaming mug of coffee, sugar, cream, and a plate of cookies. Smiling, he knocked. ''Room service,'' he said, then turned the knob and stepped inside—directly into the path of a flying pillow.

''*You* drink the coffee!'' Whizzing past him, fully dressed and suitcase in hand, Sarina paused. ''And I hope you choke on it!''

Licking his burned fingers, Max set the tray and its spilled contents on the bed, then tore after Sarina. ''Have you lost your mind?''

''I've just found it,'' she shouted, getting down on her knees and searching under the sofa for her hiking boots.

Max got down beside her. ''What is the matter with you?''

One boot in hand, she looked at him. '''You've changed me completely, Sarina. I'm a new man,''' she said, mimicking him. ''Liar!''

''What's the matter out here?'' Rance stood in the doorway of the other bedroom.

Sarina shot up. ''I'll tell you what's the matter.'' She pointed to Max. ''*He's* not gay!''

Hands on hips, Max gaped at her. ''Gay?''

''Max is gay?'' Jillian ducked beneath her husband's arm. ''I knew something funny was going on between you two!''

Max glared at Jillian. ''I am not gay!''

''I'll say you're not,'' Sarina yelled as she stomped about, searching for her other boot. ''Weirdo!''

As Sarina scoured beneath the sofa, Max fixed narrow sights on her rear end. ''Let me kick this around a minute,'' he said. "You're mad at me because I'm *not* gay and you're saying *I'm* weird?"

Scrambling to her feet, boot in hand, Sarina charged at him, hobbling. "What would you call it when a straight man goes to a woman's apartment in the middle of the night dressed in a peignoir?"

"You wore a peignoir to her apartment?" Rance turned to his wife. "And you think some of the things I ask you to wear are strange."

"Do you mind, Dokter? This is between Sarina and me." Max turned to find Sarina seated, lacing up her boots. "I told you I could explain that, only not just then."

"Yes, and now I know why."

Max caged her. "Not unless you know my partner was having me followed."

"Oh, did you rip him off, too?"

Utterly frustrated, Max stood up and spread his arms wide. "I haven't ripped anybody off!"

"Not much," Sarina said, rising. She feinted to the left and when he matched her move, she escaped right, shouting over her shoulder, "I have to admit, pretending to be gay is the most novel strategy I've ever heard of for getting a woman into bed."

"Gee," Rance said. "I wish I'd thought of that."

"So do I," Max shouted. "At least then Sarina would have a right to be angry with me!"

"Nice try, Max," Sarina shouted back. "But I can see now that every move you made in our relationship was just a carefully crafted part of your devious plot to add me to your trophy case."

Max held his hands up. "Okay, you're right, Sarina. I did such a great job trying to deceive you into bed that I must have deceived myself, too, because I didn't know that that was what I was doing."

"I'll tell you what you *did* know," Sarina shot back. "You knew from our conversation that first day in my office that I didn't trust men. You knew you couldn't take the usual route into my bed, so, when you realized I thought you were gay, you must have thanked your stars. What better way to get me to lower my guard than to let me go on thinking you were incapable of wanting sex with me? After that, you waited patiently, alert for just the right moment to flatter me into thinking I'd changed you. Then, according to your sick logic, I'd have no choice but to let you make love to me.''

Bending over, she picked up her suitcase. "There was just one thing you didn't figure on, Max. That I'd be more worried about what the sudden switch would do to you than I'd be flattered by discovering the power of my feminine charms. You see, I really did love you.''

As she headed to the door, Max caught her wrist. "You've never been more wrong about anything in your life, Sarina. I admit I was incredibly attracted to you the moment I laid eyes on you, but I had no grand strategy to get you into bed. Just the opposite. For reasons I don't want to go into right now, I was trying my damnedest not to think of you that way. You say you thought I was gay, and I can see now why you did. But I never had any idea that's what you thought. You've got to believe me.''

"You know what I believe?" Sarina replied, wrenching her hand from his grip and reaching into the pocket of her jeans. "These.''

Max ducked the small box she threw in his face. Hearing it hit the floor behind him, he turned and stooped to pick it up. "Oh, no," he said, seeing the package of condoms he'd bought less than a few hours ago. "Sarina, you don't understand," he said, facing her. "I didn't bring these with me from the city. I bought them here, tonight.''

"I guess I was wrong, then," she said bitterly. "About there being just *one* thing you hadn't thought of.''

Standing beside Sarina, Rance put his arm comfortingly

about her shoulder. "Don't you worry, Sarina. Pumpkin and I will take you home."

Coming to Sarina's other side, Jillian gave Max a disgusted look. "All I can say is, what a rotten thing to do on Valentine's Day."

"Valentine's Day?" Sarina hadn't realized until now that it was 1:00 A.M. on Sunday, the fourteenth of February. But the Hex, apparently, was as mindful of special occasions as ever. If this was any preview, she shuddered to think what the curse had planned for her birthday in less than a month. At the same time, it was hard to imagine that whatever happened, it could be much worse than this. From long practice, she forced herself to swallow her tears, then ran out the door.

ON MONDAY MORNING, sitting in his office at Friends in High Places, Max slammed down the phone. He'd lost track of the number of times he'd called Sarina in the last twenty-four hours, both at home and at work, and gotten nothing but her voice mail. Obviously, it was useless leaving any more messages. She hadn't returned one of them. She hadn't responded to her doorbell, either, nor to his requests for clearance when he'd visited the Global Century Building. He couldn't even confirm she'd arrived for work. Since she'd stormed out of the chalet last night, he'd gone from bereft to frustrated to angry to blasé to despondent. Now, he was worried. He had no idea where she was or with whom, or even if she was safe. At the moment, he'd be grateful just to know she was safe.

The phone rang. Max dived at it. "Sarina?"

"Meester Evanjeleest? Zees is Dr. Gastineaux at Ooniversity Ospital. Do you know a Meez Sarina Mann?"

Breathless, Max listened to the doctor explain in a thick French accent that Sarina had had an accident. "Is she all right?"

"Well, eet eez too soon to tell, but I'm calling because

zhere seems to be some problem with her medical insurance.''

"You listen to me, Doctor!" Max shot to his feet. "You see to it that she gets the best care, whatever it costs. I'll cover her bills myself!" Before hanging up, he told the physician he'd be right over, then grabbed his coat and tore from the room. Racing toward the main door, he pulled on his coat.

"Meester Evajeleest?"

With one coat sleeve dangling, Max turned to the voice of Dr. Gastineaux, which was suddenly right behind him. "Tony?"

Grinning, Max's brother-in-law and partner walked toward him. "If you recall, I said I'd figure out a way to prove that your Friendship with your client was more than a cold, hard business relationship. Sorry, Max."

"Sorry doesn't cut it," Max said, despite realizing Tony hadn't yet read the fax in which he'd conceded the bet. He grabbed him by the lapels of his sport coat. "Do you have any idea of the scare you gave me? How would you like it if the situation were reversed, if some joker on the other end of the phone told you your wife was in danger?"

Tony's eyes narrowed. "Max, forgive me. I had no idea how you felt about her. My God, you're actually in love with this one!"

Max let Tony go. "Yeah, and she hates the sight of me. She won't return my calls...I don't even know if she's in town."

Tony clamped Max's arm. "Is there anything I can do?"

Max gave a sad laugh. "Yeah, you can tell me the name of that lousy detective you used to follow me so I'll know to hire somebody else to track her down."

"Mr. Evangelist, it's so good to see you!"

Max turned to see the smiling face of the grandmotherly Sylvia Weinstein.

"We've really missed you around here," she said.

Max was stunned. Sylvia wasn't exactly one of his ardent supporters. In fact, he hadn't thought he had any at Friends in High Places. "You have?"

With a scolding look, she handed Tony a tall stack of papers. "You have faxes and letters more than two weeks old to answer, Tony," she said, then looked at Max. "We've been a little disorganized around here since you've been out in the field. All the Friends hope you'll be back in the office soon."

Max thanked Sylvia, not having the heart to tell her just yet that he wouldn't be back at all. He didn't work at Friends in High Places anymore.

ON HER BIRTHDAY, alone in her secret Roman garden, Sarina sat on a chaise beneath a sun that was much warmer than it had been only a few weeks ago. The ivy on the walls, the trees and the flowers weren't yet in full-bloom, but buds dotted the landscape with promise. As she set aside the reports she hadn't been able to focus on, she wondered, *promise of what? Of love?* Perhaps, but not for her. Not for the woman who had bought this hotel because she had seen it and its garden as a romantic, nurturing haven from a crass, commercial world. Bought it because she had imagined sharing it with the man she loved. Strolling the garden, fingering the sprouting twigs and branches, she ached, still, with the irony of his deception. He could have shared her love all along. She'd gladly have given it to him. Instead, he chose to play her for a damn fool. No hex had been at work, she knew, just good old-fashioned human cruelty and selfishness. Max Evangelist's, to be exact.

"Thank God. All the way over, I prayed you'd still be here."

Startled, Sarina faced the intruder. Her breath caught at the sight of him, tall and square-shouldered; thinner, perhaps, but still elegant. His face appeared a bit drawn, with a shadowy stubble, and dark half circles smudging the flesh beneath eyes that were bright, almost feverish. He had the look of a man on a mission, one he'd complete or die trying. The look aged him a little, but in the way that makes men who've wrestled with their demons all the more attractive.

Damn you, Max. "You could have saved yourself—and God—the trouble," Sarina said, gathering her reports and stalking past him.

He caught her arm, turning her toward him. "I'm not letting you get away, not this time. At least not until you read this." Still holding onto her, he removed an envelope from inside his jacket.

Sarina refused to look at it, much less take it from him. "You're wasting your time," she said, wresting her arm from his grasp. "Nothing you have to say is of any interest to me."

"You've made that quite clear," Max replied. "But I didn't write this letter. Nick DeGrasso did and you're going to hear what he has to say if I have to tie you down and read it to you myself."

Sarina's gaze dropped to the cream-colored envelope with her parish's return address printed in the upper left corner. "So, that's how you found me." Her brows shirred. "How would you know Father Nick?"

"You mean, why would a good guy like Nick hang out with a sinner like me?" Max shrugged. "Following his boss's example, I guess."

Sarina looked away, then cocked a hard stare at Max. "Then I suggest you seek his professional help with forgiveness. I'm just not very good at it."

As she stepped away, Max turned toward her. "At giving it or asking for it?"

Halting, Sarina looked at him in astonishment. His stance was wide, almost arrogant as he slapped the envelope against the palm of his hand. "Are you suggesting that *I* should ask *you* for forgiveness?"

"That's usually what people do when they jump to wrong conclusions," he replied, shouldering toward her. He looked at the envelope then thrust it at her once more. "It's all in here, Sarina. Father Nick knows all about us. When you told him you were leaving for Rome because you'd been betrayed by a man you'd thought was a friend, a man you'd hired to be your friend, he realized you were the anonymous woman I'd been talking to him about for weeks. The woman who was keeping me awake nights."

"Oh?" Lifting her chin, Sarina folded her arms. "And does he know *why* I was keeping you awake nights? Does he know that you stayed up scheming to conceal your sexual intentions toward me under the guise of friendship?"

A wise-guy smile tugged at one corner of Max's mouth. "Actually, he does."

Sarina studied the envelope. She'd always trusted her pastor, but now, she felt even he had betrayed her. "Why should I believe what's in that letter, when I asked Father Nick not to tell anyone where I was?"

"He didn't tell me, at least not in so many words," Max replied, stepping closer, so close, Sarina gasped for air. "He called me in the middle of the night and said he could no longer counsel me about the woman who was keeping us both awake nights because he'd just discovered she was a parishioner. I asked him where you were, he refused to tell me. Then, he wished me luck and said, '*Arrivederci,* Max.'"

Sarina snorted. "Collar or not, you men really stick together, don't you? I think Father Nick had it right, though. *Arrivederci,* Max." Turning, she walked toward the hotel.

She never made it to the entrance. Taking her by the arm, Max reeled her toward him. Her papers scattered as he swept her up and carried her toward the chaise.

"Kick all you want, Sarina," he said. "You're still going to hear what the good Father has to say." He deposited her on the chaise and when she struggled to get away, he

pinned her back, holding her wrists down. "I mean business, Sarina, and this is one time you won't be able to
negotiate your way out."

Breathing hard, she glared up at him. "You phony. Don't
you see that I could only believe that you fooled Father
Nick the way you fooled me? You can read his letter, Max,
but you can't make me trust that a word of it is grounded
in truth."

Max lowered himself toward her, his lips hovering over
hers. "I think I can," he murmured, smiling, "with a little
friendly persuasion."

Swiftly, he claimed her mouth, his kiss a sear that threat-
ened to burn away the layers of Sarina's defenses. When
his hands released hers and caressed her shoulders, she
pushed against his chest and gurgled noises of protest that
only made him deepen his kiss. His tongue consumed hers,
turning her protests into whimpers of pleasure. Then she
felt his palms mold themselves to her breasts, go flat as
they circled her nipples, then press along her torso and slip
beneath her hips. Her arms fell limply to the chaise. She
was out of breath—and out of reasons not to read Father
Nick's letter.

Sensing her submission, Max stood up. For the second
time, he took the letter from inside his jacket pocket.
"Please, Sarina," he said. Then, dropping the letter on the
chaise, he walked away, disappearing in a stand of trees in
the most secluded corner of the garden.

More confused now than mistrustful, Sarina opened the
envelope. As she read its contents, she occasionally glanced
in bewilderment toward the small arbor that concealed Max
from her view. Once, she laughed out loud. But by the time
she came to the final sentence, she was reading through
tears. Dropping the sheets of paper on the chaise, she ran
toward the far corner of the garden and entered the arbor
beneath a green, fragrant canopy. She saw Max ahead, his

broad back to her. Tiptoeing up behind him, she slipped her arms around his waist.

"Father Nick tells me all about the bet you had with your brother-in-law," she said. "And that the night you came to my apartment in drag, you were trying to evade Tony's investigator."

"To tell you the truth," he replied, "my ego was deflated because he didn't follow me. I thought I looked pretty sexy."

Sarina smiled. "If I remember correctly, so did Jack."

Max covered her hands with his own. "What can I say? I'm a man with broad appeal."

"Yeah?" Sarina gave him a squeeze. "Well, from now on, you'll have to limit your appeal to just one broad."

Max turned around, taking her by the shoulders. "And who would that be?"

"The one Father Nick said you gave up the agency for that night in the Catskills. He said you loved her so much you'd rather lose your business than her respect, and you'd planned to tell her so that same night." Sarina circled her arms around his neck. "But he didn't expect me to take his word for it. He enclosed a copy of the fax you showed him, the one you sent Tony *before* you came back to the lodge."

Clamping his arms around her, Max began a gentle swaying. "Well, I suppose Nick's used to dealing with skeptics."

"That reminds me. There's still one thing I'm skeptical about," Sarina said, a Cheshire-cat grin on her face. "Father Nick says there's something you want to ask me. I wonder what it could be."

Max held her away from him. "You'll have to wonder a little longer," he said. Then, tapping the pocket on the side of his jacket, "Take a look."

"Oh, no," Sarina replied, shaking her head. "I made the mistake of looking in one of your pockets before." She walked deeper in the small arbor and sat on the ground. Curling her legs beneath her, she plucked a blade of grass.

Max sat down beside her. "Let's just say I'd like to make up for that." Sliding his fingers beneath hers, he clasped them. "Besides, it's your birthday."

Looking up at him, Sarina laughed with incredulity. "All the more reason not to. The Mann Hex never rests."

Max gazed deeply into her eyes. "The only curse on you, Sarina, is the curse of living without trust. Dispel it, Angel," he whispered, holding open his pocket, "once and for all."

Slowly, her eyes never leaving his, Sarina put her hand inside his pocket. Her fingers touched something small and possibly porcelain. She removed it and set it in the palm of her hand.

"It's a cherub," she said, delighting at the dimpled, naughty smile playing around its mouth. Then, seeing a slender gold ribbon around its white neck, she turned the little angel around. Between its wings dangled a radiant, round solitaire diamond ring. Sarina's wide-eyed gaze flew to Max's.

"It may not be large enough to have to keep in a vault," he said, removing it from the ribbon, "but my love is. That vault." He looked heavenward.

Sarina followed his gaze, glimpsing celestial blue through a patchwork of green. When Max took her left hand, she looked down and watched as he slipped the ring over her third finger. He stopped midway, drawing her gaze to his.

"Will you marry me, Angel?"

Sarina didn't answer. She merely guided his hand—and the ring—to the base of her finger. When she looked up at him, she knew the light in her eyes must be miraculous because it came from the love in her heart. Slowly, she lay back on the sweet, warm earth. She held her arms out to Max, out to the man she loved and trusted.

"Come, darling. Come into my garden."

Epilogue

FATHER NICK DEGRASSO shook the hands of the two people he had just blessed in marriage. As they began to express their gratitude, he stopped them. "I'm the one who's grateful. Now I can look forward to sleeping through the night again." With an irrepressible grin, he gazed out at the congregation. "Ladies and gentlemen, it is my great privilege to present Mr. and Mrs. Max Evangelist."

Turning toward the applause, Max and Sarina accepted the congratulations of the two people who'd stood up with them, Tony and Dr. Barrett Brown. Max had an especially warm, understanding smile of friendship for his best man, who'd given him the torn pieces of his original fax as a gift the night of his bachelor party. He had no doubt he and Tony would make an even greater success of the agency—together. Sarina shared a gleeful hug with her former therapist and matron of honor, who was radiantly pregnant. As Max shook hands with his other groomsman, a pal from the past whose friendship he'd recently renewed, Sarina exchanged a hug and sisterly words with her other bridesmaid, Max's sister Mike.

Walking up the aisle, they shared smiles with the friends and loved ones who had gathered to wish them well. The gangs from Global Century and Friends in High Places were there. So were Rance and Jillian, Jack and his new love, and Dr. Barrett Brown's husband, Henley, who was rocking Mike and Tony's baby boy.

The sun, Sarina noted, streamed in a rainbow through

the stained-glass windows, and all was right with the world. Too right.

On the way back to her apartment, where she and Max planned to relax between their wedding mass and the formal reception, she grew anxious. By the time they picked up her mail, she was wringing her hands. Now, standing outside her door as Max unlocked it, she was near panic. She pressed her palm to his tuxedoed chest. "Wait, Max. I know our new apartment won't be ready until we get back from our honeymoon in Italy and technically this isn't our threshold, but I think you'd better carry me across it anyway. I don't want anything to go wrong."

Shaking his head and handing her the mail, Max stooped to lift her. "When we got engaged on your birthday, I thought you agreed there is no curse on your family's weddings," he said as he carried her into the foyer, kicking the door behind him.

"I thought so, too," she replied as he set her down. "And you're right. From Great-Great-Grandfather Mann forward, every disastrous wedding has led to a disastrous marriage because the two people were completely unsuited to each other. So, if there was a hobgoblin at work, it was like mine, a tiny inner voice that tried to warn me I was about to marry the wrong man."

Max drew her into his embrace. "And have you heard any inner voices today?"

Sarina listened in silence, then laughed at herself. "No," she said, hooking her arms under his, inviting his kiss and receiving it. It grew so deep and demanding, she felt herself lifted off the floor. Soon, she could see the mail in her hand behind his shoulder. *"Hmmmmm!"*

"What?" Max set her down. "Why did you scream?"

Her eyes bugging, Sarina poked her finger at the top envelope in the stack. "You see, I told you something would go wrong. It's the curse! Oh, Max," she cried, turning away. "Maybe our marriage was a horrible mistake."

Taking a breath, Max snatched the stack from her, tossing all but the first letter on the chair. His brows arched when he read the return address. "Internal Revenue Service?"

"I'm being audited, I just know it." Sarina clutched her throat. "My accountant is probably a crook and I owe the government millions in back taxes. I'll go to jail! Max," she cried, facing him, "will you wait for me?"

He stood with his arms folded, the contents of the envelope dangling from the fingers of one hand. "Sorry, Angel. I know Bogie promised Mary Astor he'd be there when she got out of the joint, but—"

"*The Maltese Falcon,* 1941." She gave him a forlorn look. "So, you won't wait?"

With a stern expression, he shook his head. "You'd better read this."

Her hand trembling, Sarina took the letter. Three seconds later, her head shot up. Flinging the sheet in the air, she leaped into his arms. "I'm not going to jail. I'm getting a refund!"

Holding her aloft, Max turned toward the bedroom. "Tell me again, how much time have we got?"

Sarina clasped her arms around his neck and smiled. "Forever."

The last thing she heard before Max shut the bedroom door behind them was a soft, proud voice inside her heart.

Bye, Sarina. May you and Max always walk with angels.

shocking pink

THEY WERE ONLY WATCHING…

The mysterious lovers the three girls spied on were engaged in a deadly sexual game no one else was supposed to know about. Especially not Andie and her friends whose curiosity had deepened into a dangerous obsession….

Now fifteen years later, Andie is being watched by someone who won't let her forget the unsolved murder of "Mrs. X" or the sudden disappearance of "Mr. X." And Andie doesn't know who her friends are….

WHAT THEY SAW WAS MURDER.

ERICA SPINDLER

Available in February 1998 at your favorite retail outlet.

The Brightest Stars in Women's Fiction.™

DEBBIE MACOMBER

invites you to the

HEART OF TEXAS

Join Debbie Macomber as she brings you the lives
and loves of the folks in the ranching community
of Promise, Texas.

If you loved Midnight Sons—don't miss
Heart of Texas! A brand-new six-book series
from Debbie Macomber.

Available in February 1998
at your favorite retail store.

Heart of Texas by Debbie Macomber

Lonesome Cowboy	February '98
Texas Two-Step	March '98
Caroline's Child	April '98
Dr. Texas	May '98
Nell's Cowboy	June '98
Lone Star Baby	July '98

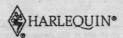

HARLEQUIN®

HPHRT1

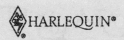

Not The Same Old Story!

Exciting, glamorous romance stories that take readers around the world.

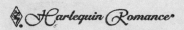
Sparkling, fresh and tender love stories that bring you pure romance.

Bold and adventurous— Temptation is strong women, bad boys, great sex!

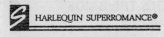
Provocative and realistic stories that celebrate life and love.

Contemporary fairy tales—where anything is possible and where dreams come true.

Heart-stopping, suspenseful adventures that combine the best of romance and mystery.

Humorous and romantic stories that capture the lighter side of love.